ROUGH RIDE

SCREAMING DEMONS MC
BOOK TWO

SUMMER COOPER
SIENNA CHANCE

LOVY BOOKS

Kye watched Eliana out of the corner of his eye. She was staring open-mouthed at the buildings as they passed through downtown Pine Hill.

"A lot has changed," Kye said, echoing her thoughts. It was dark now, but the town was lit up. Whereas when she'd left there was a single stoplight town, they now boasted nearly twenty and the former mom-and-pop shops were either sporting an upgraded vintage look or had been overtaken by local franchises.

While Pine Hill would never be a booming metropolis, they had certainly seen more advancement than Eliana was anticipating. The streets were freshly paved, they now had localized apartment buildings with quaint balconies. Considering it was nearly ten at night, the streets were busy with people walking, riding bicycles, or motorcycles. A movie theater was just letting out, and when Kye stopped at a red light, Eliana saw there was an outdoor patio in front of a new bowling alley.

"I don't even recognize the place," she said with a sense of nostalgia. Kye drove directly through downtown, and Eliana noted the only two places that were still untouched by time were the diner and the bar her dad spent most of his time at.

The town fell behind them as they moved through the city and to the outskirts where Kye took a sharp left. Less than a mile down the road, a large metal beam crossed overhead, and the sign read 'Hell Hollow Road' with the Screaming Demon logo. Eliana felt a wave of fear overtake her. All around her was blackness, and pine trees loomed like sentries in the night.

Every so many feet, another metal sign would read something like 'Keep Out', 'Enter at your own risk,' 'Private Property', 'Turn back or die' with a skull and bones spray-painted on it. Every reasonable bone in her body knew it was for dramatic effect, but at the present, it was entirely convincing. Eliana had read Dante's Inferno for school, and at the moment she couldn't help but make the correlation that she was entering the first circle of hell.

In the back of her mind, she knew she was headed toward the abandoned steel mill, but the transformation of the property was anything but vacant. The tree line opened, and in the distance she saw the large metal compound encircled by a chain-link fence topped with barbed wire. Several new additions had been built, two of which looked like housing, and the others were lit up like an onsite bar.

As they drew near, Eliana could hear the commotion of dozens of people who were flocked to the center of the hub that was built like a courtyard. Tables and chairs were placed outside the bar, and nearly sixty motorcycles were parked outside. Music was blasting and even from inside the car, Eliana could feel the vibrations of the ground.

Kye pulled the car to a stop in the makeshift parking lot behind the bar and quickly exited. He stretched his arms high over his head, clearly eager to be out of the car they'd been in the last eight hours, but as the back of his shirt lifted, Eliana caught sight of the holster and gun he had on his left hip. From his seated position in the car, she'd missed it.

Frank and Bruce were right behind them, and they pulled their bikes up to the left side of the car. Kye said something to them that she couldn't hear over the raucous noise, and all three laughed. They dismounted their bikes and moved toward the building where several people were standing outside smoking and drinking. In fact, if Eliana had seen correctly, one man was peeing into a beer bottle while two other men egged him on.

Frozen to her seat, Eliana refused to get out when Kye waved to her. He frowned and moved around to her side of the door.

"Get out of the car, Eli," he instructed, and she shook her head. He reached for the handle, but this time she was faster than him and locked it. He sighed and pinched the bridge of his nose. "You're being ridiculous; I still have the keys," he said and pressed the unlock button.

Eliana locked it again.

"Stop it," Kye said and pressed the button once again. Eliana hit the lock. Kye pounded his fist on the window, and she jumped. "Unlock the door!"

"No."

"You're being childish."

"I'm not getting out."

"I'll break the window."

"It's your car, what do I care?"

"Eliana," Kye warned. His tone was far more serious than she'd ever heard him use before. She stared hard into his eyes and let out a shaky breath before unlocking the door. Kye opened it for her and took her by the arm to help her out. "Thank you," he said, leading her away from the door.

"Wait," she said and pulled her arm away. Kye could

see she was shaking in fear. The culmination of the last ten years of always looking over her shoulder, trying to stay under the radar, always worrying that someone was coming for them, had clearly taken its toll. The overwhelming surroundings likely weren't helping her. While Kye had long-since gotten used to the rowdy gang and hordes of Wall Kats, Hell Kats, Groupies and Gear Nuts that kept the headquarters hopping, Eliana looked entirely freaked out.

"Come here," Kye said, reaching for her hand. She took it and stepped toward him. "You'll be fine," he said and began unbuttoning his shirt. "Just stay close to me, and you'll be fine." He popped the trunk of the car and tossed his white shirt in the back and took out his leather cut that was folded in the back. He then pulled it on over the wife-beater undershirt he'd been wearing under his dress shirt. Eliana's observation of his toned chest was confirmed when she saw the way his pectorals stood out under the thin fabric. How many pushups did this guy do in a day?

"Where have you been all day?" a familiar-looking, blond man asked as he approached from the opposite side of the car. Kye closed the trunk, and the curly-haired man looked from Kye to Eliana, and his eyes widened. "No shit."

"Grier," Kye said in a reprimanding tone and glared at him. "It's not what you think."

"Doesn't matter what I think," Grier said, but he still looked vastly amused. "I never thought you'd actually go after her. Dude, it's been like a decade. You're still hung up on her?"

"Believe it or not, this isn't personal— it's business," Kye said, turning his back to Eliana to face Grier. Eliana vaguely remembered the boy who had come to her rescue in the diner and walked her home afterward. He'd spent the entire walk trying to explain Kye's fragile position in the gang and some of the more tedious and dangerous semantics of being a Demon. At the time, it had abated her temper at Kye's perceived apathy, but now as the two spoke about her as though she wasn't standing there, she felt anger welling up in her.

"Business? As in old business?" Grier asked with raised eyebrows. "Damn, Max sure can hold a grudge."

"I have a feeling this has more to do with me, than her," Kye said in a lowered tone, but Eliana heard.

"You need backup?"

"Probably better not. I don't want Max losing his shit when I walk in with an entourage. I think he wants to ensure he's got the upper hand, but thanks."

"Anytime. You going to take her in there looking like that?"

"What's wrong with how I look?" Eliana chimed in, feeling like she could no longer hold her tongue. Both of them turned to face her, and she placed both hands on her hips. Grier looked her up and down and grinned.

"Not a damn thing, Cherry," Grier teased, and Kye smacked him on the chest. "Sorry, sorry," he feigned with raised hands. "Do yourself a favor and get a drink in her before you go see Max. She's a little wound up."

"Wound up? I am not wound up!" Eliana stepped toward him, but Kye wrapped an arm around her shoulders.

"Come on, Eli," Kye said and led her toward the tin shack that served as a bar. Eliana tossed a glare over her shoulder at Grier before facing the direction they were walking. While she didn't appreciate his insinuation, the moment they stepped inside, Eliana couldn't help feeling he may have been on to something.

She'd opted for a comfortable pair of dark denim skinny jeans, her practical but stylish cream-colored wedges and a green satin blouse with decorative buttons on the sleeves and a tan leather jacket over. It was something she would have worn to a Saturday brunch with the girls or a business casual meeting with colleagues. Too bad she hadn't tapped into her 'kidnapped into a den of bikers' wardrobe. The entire occupancy of the bar turned to face them and stare when they walked in.

Eliana could feel the scrutiny draped on her like a wet blanket. She clearly didn't belong, even with Kye's arm still around her. Where she looked vanilla, the women in this place were cinnamon. Fishnets. Short-shorts. Sky-high boots. Leather. Red lipstick. Low cut tops and big breasts.

Eliana felt like a Catholic nun in comparison.

Her face flushed hot, and she was grateful when Kye led her farther toward the bar. She quickly ducked onto the free stool and placed a hand over the side of her face that wasn't directed toward Kye. "What are we doing in here? Is this where we're meeting Max?" she asked in a hushed tone that was entirely unnecessary. The rock music that was playing over the jukebox would have provided enough noise to cover their conversation.

"Grier doesn't usually have good ideas, but this one I agree with," Kye stated and waved the bartender over. She was a tall woman, probably pushing six feet, with long, fire-engine red hair she wore in a single braid down her back. Her skin was flawlessly tan, and she had a mole under her left eye. Dressed in leather pants that fit like a second layer of skin and a tank top that read "Hell Kat" in blue lettering, she also sported a headband with two cat ears that looked more like horns. "Jez," Kye said, and the woman, who was likely in her late forties, leaned over the bar, her breasts plopping firmly on the wooden counter, and kissed Kye directly on the mouth.

"KD, good to see you," she said in a smoke-ridden husky voice that oozed sex appeal. "How was Ireland?"

"Rainy," Kye said and kissed the back of Jez's hand. Eliana's jaw made a clicking sound. "Max around?"

"In his office, but he told me that if I saw you to send you on to him. He been expecting you?"

"Yeah," Kye answered shortly. Jez looked from Kye to Eliana, her dark blue eyes assessing her like a teacher would a new student.

"Who's the girl?"

"Jez, this is Eliana, Eli this is Jez. She runs the bar and keeps the Hell Kats in line," Kye explained. Eliana extended her hand, and Jez hesitated before taking it. Her grip was as crushing as a vice.

"Speaking of, Ebony has been missing you," Jez said to Kye but kept her eyes on Eliana without releasing her hand. "Should I send her your way tonight?"

"Uh no, no, that's not necessary," Kye said quickly and scratched the back of his neck. "Just tell her I'll call her later."

"Sure thing, doll," Jez replied and turned Eliana's hand over in hers to examine her palm. "You haven't worked much, have you?"

"That would depend on your definition of work," Eliana said sharply and pulled her hand away. Jez laughed and reached for the bottle opener on her belt.

"I like her," Jez said, looking back at Kye before she popped the lids to two cold beers she then placed in front of them. "Drink up then go see Max. I don't want him thinking I'm the reason you're late," Jez said, pointing a warning finger at Kye.

"We're in and out," Kye promised and took a swig of beer. Jez leaned over the counter again, her large breasts making her neck disappear as they pushed upward.

"Do us a favor, sweet-thing, get changed before you see him. You're caked in mud, lookin' like shit, and smelling twice as bad."

"You always say the nicest things," Kye teased and kissed Jez on the cheek before grabbing his beer and standing. "Still got some things in the back?"

"My office," she answered with a nod toward the corner.

"Stay right here," Kye said to Eliana, and she opened her mouth to say something, but before she could, he was moving through the crowd. Closing her mouth, she wrapped both hands around her bottle and faced the bar, hoping the rest of the room would leave her alone. She looked up when she felt Jez staring at her.

"What?" she asked as the redhead smirked.

"He likes you," Jez said, crossing her arms.

"Who?"

"Don't play dumb," Jez scolded with slightly narrowed eyes. "We both know you're not."

"I don't think you know anything about me," Eliana stated frankly, and Jez's perfectly sculpted eyebrows rose.

"I'm a pretty good judge of people," she said with an air of pride. "I know you're small town. You've got that goody-goody vibe."

"It's Pine Hill, we're all small town."

"I know you've got soft hands so you work at a desk, but you bite your nails, so it's something stressful. Stockbroker?"

"Lawyer."

"Even worse," Jez said and took Eliana's beer from her. When Eliana's brow furrowed, Jez took a long swig. "We don't waste good beer in this place."

"I prefer bourbon."

"No, you don't," Jez said with a coy smile. "You're a whiskey girl playing at bourbon." Jez reached for the top shelf and filled two glasses with Johnny Walker Black Label. Eliana took the one handed to her and slammed it. The liquid burned, and she coughed a couple of times much to Jez's amusement. The older woman downed hers in one long gulp and smiled before pouring them both another one.

"So you've got me all figured out," Eliana said sarcastically. "Tell me, what exactly does a Hell Kat do?" Her question was biting, but Jez played along.

"You see him?" she asked, pointing to a man in the center of the room. He was surrounded by a crowd of men and women who were all listening to him ramble on. He must have said something funny because the crowd laughed.

"Yeah."

"We do things like him. That's Riggs. One of the Demon Elite."

"So you're prostitutes?" Eliana asked, looking back at Jez whose smile turned to a frown.

"Hookers get paid, little girl," Jez said coldly. "Around here, being a Hell Kat is like royalty. Some girls spend their entire lives on the Wall and never get promoted. We get respect and prestige. That's something your fancy law degree won't get you around here."

"What are you two talking about?" Kye asked, breaking the conversation. He was dressed in clean jeans and had brushed his hair and let it down from his ponytail. He smelled of a potent and alluring cologne.

"Status," Jez said before Eliana could say anything.

"Oh," Kye said, not fully understanding. He set his empty beer bottle on the bar. "Anyway, we need to go," he said to Eliana. "Max is waiting." Eliana let out a shaking breath and looked from Kye to Jez and knocked back her second shot of whiskey.

"Now or never."

2

*E*liana thought she would feel relieved to be out of the bar and away from Jez's interrogation, but as they crossed the courtyard, her stomach that was filled with nothing but top-shelf whiskey, knotted itself with nerves. The large building that they entered was the renovated warehouse that had served as the main building for the steel mill. The floor was cement, though it looked like it had recently been polished.

Surprisingly, the place had been arranged with care. Clearly reserved for the men of the club, there was an L-shaped bar and kitchen to her right where currently no one was and across from that, separated by several benches, was a gym with fairly high-tech equipment. To their left, a large common room had been set up complete with couches, armchairs, four televisions, three octagonal poker tables and chairs, as well as book-shelves lining the wall.

Next to the bookshelves were four floor-to-ceiling garage doors that were currently closed but led to the adjoining building they used as a maintenance shop for their vehicles. The whole place looked expertly reno-vated, including lighting fixtures, a walled-in bathroom, and even decorations. The only remaining evidence in the place had been a factory where the chains and gear tracks still hung from the ceiling.

"This way," Kye said, placing a hand on her back and leading her toward the room. "Max's office is upstairs." Eliana only nodded. While outside had felt like a Friday night at the county fair, the ambiance of the clubhouse was that of a stag room in a men's only club. The only thing missing were antlers on the walls and red-vested man in the corner named Horatio who clipped the tips of cigars and called everyone 'master'.

The few men who were inside were using the gym, and their bare chests and rippled abdomens were covered in sweat. They looked at Kye then Eliana with a mixture of curiosity and hunger. She quickly turned her eyes toward the single door on the far end of the room where she was being led.

If Hell Hollow Road was the first circle of hell, the bar was definitely the lust-filled second level. With the markings of indulgence so evident in the warehouse,

Eliana felt the walls screaming gluttony which would make this the fourth. How many levels would she find on the other side of this steel door?

Without much time to anticipate it, Kye opened the door and let her step in first. Looking more like the sterile corridor of a hospital, only fluorescent lights lit the windowless passage. She couldn't help but drag her feet, and Kye had to take her by the hand to keep her moving. When they reached the end of the hallway, they trekked up a staircase.

At the top, another shorter hallway led the opposite direction giving the implication that the office overlooked the warehouse below them. The hall opened into a makeshift waiting room where four men were sitting around a foldout table chatting. They all stopped and stood. Dressed in jeans, black shirts, and patched leather cuts, Eliana could see their guns openly displayed on their hips.

Two of the men had long, ponytail bound hair, one had a crew cut that screamed 'former military', and the other chose to shave his dark head bald. Eliana didn't think it was possible for Frank and Bruce to be dwarfed, but this special-forces-looking-crew had enough testosterone to produce a dozen men.

"Here to see Max, KD?" the crewcut man asked and spit a mouthful of sunflower seeds into an ashtray.

"He's expecting us," Kye replied. Crewcut poured

another handful of shell-covered seeds into his mouth before rapping twice on the heavy, dark wood door. The only indication he had heard from someone was the way he tilted his head to the right where a coil cord connected to an earpiece.

"Go ahead," he said with a bulging cheek and opened the door. The two men with ponytails entered first, and Kye's nudge on her back urged her in behind them. When Kye reached the doorway, Crewcut placed a hand on his shoulder. "Not you."

"Kye?" Eliana asked when she realized he wasn't behind her. Seeing he was still standing in the door-way, his blank expression was only disrupted by the slightly panicked and apologetic look in his eyes. Before she could chime in a protest, the door slammed shut. It might as well have been the slamming of a coffin door.

"Miss," the man to her left said and gestured for her to move farther into the room. As she did, the two of them took their place on either side of the door effectively barring her exit.

In the complete contrast to the foldout table, chairs, and cement floor of the room she'd just entered from, this office was like the cover of a Forbes magazine. The carpet was a short-cropped white that made her worry she was tracking mud. The walls were also white with marble textured reflective flecks of gold. In front of her was an alabaster desk with only a single white leather chair behind it.

To her right was an L-shaped chaise lounge sectional with an all leather, cylindrical resting table in the center. A wooden tray with a decanter of amber liquid and four glasses was the only color the formal sitting area offered. What drew her attention, however, was the gray-marble sculpture in the corner.

The six-foot figurine was a large, flawlessly polished hand whose fingers cradled a bird with intricately carved feathers. The hand was in a slightly strained position, and yet its fingers were not coiled around the bird. Rather it cradled with surprising gentleness considering the powerful figurine. She was still staring at it when the door on the left side of the room slammed open and startled her.

"Do you have any idea how hard it is to take a piss toting this piece of shit around?" A man with gray hair emerged from the office bathroom carting a wheeled oxygen tank behind him. He was tall, around Kye's height, possibly taller, but the way he stooped to pull the tank made it hard to discern. He had thick hair he kept trim and despite obviously having health issues, the muscles in his arms and hulk of his abdomen were evident in the fitted shirt he wore.

Despite his earlier question, Eliana remained silent as the man took a seat behind his desk and pulled the air tube from his nose before taking up the cigar that had been resting on the glass tray on his desk.

"Miss Granville, I presume?" he asked rhetorically as he leaned back in his chair and examined her.

"As ordered," she retorted, and he smiled in amusement. "Max Strong, is it? Or do you prefer 'your highness'?"

"Max will do just fine, as long as you mind your manners," he said, flicking a bit of ash on the tray. "I see you're admiring my statue," he observed, his thick Southern accent sounding more prominent. Clearly, he hailed from Tennessee or Kentucky by the sounds of it.

"It's beautiful," she admitted and glanced back at it. "I'm not familiar with the artist, though."

"Oh, you likely wouldn't be," he stated. "It's a local talent. Some young kid from the community school. In fact, all my pieces are bought or commissioned from the local school." He held his hand out indicating the framed pieces around the room. The colored abstract paintings complete with sculpture and ornate bookends on the desk made quite the collection.

"That's charitable," Eliana said, still rooted to her position.

"You sound surprised."

"Hate to break it to you, but your reputation doesn't scream 'local-do-gooder'," she said, tossing a glare in his direction.

"There's a town full of people out there who would disagree with you," Max said, setting his cigar down again. "Maybe I'm not the villain you think I am."

"Maybe you're exactly who I think you are," she countered with both eyebrows raised. He grinned again and stood to walk around the desk toward her.

"Do you know what this piece is called?" he asked as he stood next to her, his presence not nearly as sickly as she would have expected from a man on oxygen. "Power," he said, answering his own question. "You see, the artist understood the nature of authority. Like a bird, it's fragile, elusive, and at any time it can just… fly away," he explained with a wave of his hand.

"Yet the hand is holding it," Eliana said, not chancing to take her eyes away from Max. "That begs the question, who has the power? The bird with its ability to fly away or the hand that can hold on to it?"

"I like you, Miss Granville," Max said, smiling at her. "You're smart. You can see clearly that the bird can flee or the hand can grab. But if that hand grips too tight, he'll kill the very thing he's trying to hold on to. There's a level of understanding between the two, I think. One of the many reasons I liked it."

"So what's our understanding then?" she asked, cutting straight to the point. Max stepped just slightly closer to her, and Eliana refused to back up as he looked down at her.

"All in good time, little bird," he said in a deeper tone. Well, there was no confusion on roles in this situation. Max placed his hand on the back of her shoulder and guided her to the couch where he had her sit. "Your daddy was an enterprising man," Max began as he lifted the glass lid to the decanter and poured two glasses of the gold brandy.

"My father was a drunk and a criminal."

"There's no need to bad-mouth the dead," Max said, handing her a glass, and she was surprisingly grateful for it.

"There's no need to romanticize them either," she said, taking a sip. Max dipped his head to indicate she wasn't wrong.

"You know he had a deal worked out with some of the less reputable men from my chapters a few years ago?" Max asked as he took the seat to her right.

"I've heard a few things," Eliana replied vaguely.

"Miss Granville, it is in your best interest to be straight with me. While I like a good verbal spar with a beautiful woman, as you can see," he said, gesturing toward the oxygen tank by his desk, "my time is running short."

"I know my father was conning contracts with the lumber suppliers. He was charging commission for deliveries based on miles of road while transporting on the train line. I know he was working with a man named Dean to use a boxcar on the train to tote the lumber trucks. In return, the cars would ride back with stolen goods my dad would drop off. I don't know where or what the items were. Until the night we were run out of town, I didn't know my dad was involved with anything to do with the Screaming Demons."

"Am I supposed to believe that? Your daddy would come home with more money than any shit blue-collar job could ever pay, and you thought, what? He got lucky on some gas station scratch tickets?"

"There was never any money around the house," Eliana replied defensively. "The fridge was usually empty, and bills would pile up until I begged him to pay them. I worked summers just to provide."

"What about your house? Who paid for that? Four-bedroom, three-story house in the suburbs?"

"My dad inherited it from my mother when she died."

"What about that fancy private school? I heard you took some extra classes to get you into Ivy League."

"Scholarships and secondhand books."

"Well ain't that something," Max said, downing his drink. He leaned back in his seat and crossed his legs. "Your daddy told you all that?"

"Yes."

"Then he wasn't just a thief, he was a liar too," Max said, and Eliana felt the heat drain from her body. "Oh, don't look at me like that, Miss Granville, you must've known deep down. Your daddy didn't inherit that house, I paid for it. You didn't get into prep-school on scholarship; you got in on my dollar. Your daddy was running deliveries for the Demons since he was your age."

"That's not possible…"

"It isn't?" Max asked patronizingly. Eliana let the reality sink in before she buried her face in her hands. "If you think about it, the only reason you got into Harvard was because of me."

"My dad was working with Dean," Eliana defended with the need to have some ground to stand on.

"Who was, up until the end, a loyal member of my crew. So, you see," Max said, leaning forward, "you owe me a great deal, Miss Granville. It's time to pay up." Feeling on the verge of hyperventilating, Eliana stood and began pacing in front of his desk. Max ignored her mental breakdown and walked to his side of the desk, opened the top drawer, and removed a thick stack of files. Plopping them open on the desk, Eliana recognized the mug shots from the ones Kye had shown her.

"I'm not defending murderers," Eliana snapped. Max walked around the desk and sat on the edge of it.

"You don't have much of a choice in the matter, Miss Granville," Max said firmly. "While you are here in Pine Hill, you are at my beck-and-call. These two men are of no use to me behind bars. They're looking at the death penalty, do you know what that means?"

"They'll get what they deserve?" Eliana countered.

"No, it means they're desperate. Desperate men have a way of talking too much when they think it can benefit them. I want their case dismissed, Miss Granville. I am not accustomed to leaving loose ends. From what I understand you're a decent lawyer, and since I practically paid for that education, it's time I cashed in."

"No."

"What did you just say to me?" Max asked, standing upright.

"I said 'no'," Eliana repeated. "I'm not your servant, and I'm not their lawyer."

"You don't seem to understand the gravity of the situation, Miss Granville," Max said, stepping toward her. "I may have held you with a gentle hand, little bird, but don't think for a second I won't close my fist around you until I've choked every last ounce of life out of you." His teeth were clenched together, and with every word, he stepped closer and Eliana moved backward. Max nodded once and the two men by the door, whom she'd forgotten about entirely, each grabbed an arm, dragged her forward, and slammed her face-first onto the desk.

Crying out in pain, she felt the hand on the back of her neck, her cheek pressed against the crime files, and one arm twisted painfully behind her back. She screamed in pain again as the hand twisted more firmly.

"What will it be, Miss Granville?" Max asked, standing in front of her. Before she answered, she heard the click of two guns cocking. "Your life or theirs?"

3

Kye was doing his best not to look as nervous as he felt. While he had every confidence that Eliana was intelligent, he also knew Max's ability to break anyone down. While he leaned against the wall opposite Max's office door, the two others continued their poker game at the foldout table.

Sammy, the bald, dark-skinned man had come on board as Max's personal security only three years ago. Like Max, he'd moved north from the Southern states of the US. For the most part, he seemed like a jovial guy, but the sheer size of his biceps that looked more like the barrel end of a tank left no room for misinterpretation. This guy was lethal.

Then there was Dhal. Former Marine turned private contractor, served more tours overseas than years in the US and no one's sweetheart. While never interacting much outside of formalities, Kye knew the man had a particular distaste for him. Dhal was all meat and no charm.

"Wanna sit in a hand?" Dhal offered, and spittle from his sunflower seed-crammed mouth filled the corners of his lips. He must have been on his fourth or fifth run at quitting smoking. Last time Dhal tried to quit, two Wall Kats had turned up with bruises, and they'd had to replace one of the flat-screen TVs downstairs.

"No thanks," Kye said with his arms crossed over his chest. His eyes were still focused on the door as if mentally begging it to open, Eliana and Max to walk out laughing and hugging, claiming it was all one big misunderstanding.

"Suit yourself, KD," Dhal said, and seeing the younger man's slightly worried expression, leaned over to Sammy. "Think she's sucking his dick?" Sammy laughed at the question, and Kye's blazing eyes turned to Dhal who only shuffled the deck in his hand and began dealing out cards. "If she's smart, she'll suck his dick."

"Shut up," Kye said sternly and at the reaction, Dhal only smiled. Sammy, who didn't care in the least who won this argument, leaned back in his chair to enjoy the drama.

"Yeah, he's probably got her under that desk right now, balls deep in her mouth, a handful of hair… Think she swallows?"

"I said shut up!" Kye yelled as he grabbed the edge of the square table and flung it aside. Cards and cash went flying. Even Dhal's ashtray of spit covered, empty sunflower seed shells sprayed around the floor. Dhal sat quietly for a moment, then stood so abruptly his chair crashed to the floor behind him.

"You wanna go, pretty boy?" Dhal asked and shoved Kye's chest.

"Whatever shuts you up," Kye retorted and shoved him back. Dhal swung and hit Kye in the jaw with his rock-like fist, and Kye tackled him and landed two punches to his ribs before they hit the ground.

"Knock it off!" Sammy said, grabbing Kye by the shoulder and hoisting him to his feet. Dhal was laughing as he sat reclined on the floor, thoroughly enjoying his ability to get under Kye's skin.

"Don't worry, pretty boy, I'm sure that whore will save a mouthful for you," Dhal taunted, and Kye lunged for him again only to be held back by Sammy. That was when Kye heard Eliana scream. Shoving Sammy off, Kye vaulted over Dhal and crashed through the door to Max's office.

Eliana was bent over Max's desk, her face held firmly to the top of it by one of the other enforcers and her left arm twisted behind her back. The other man, Barret, had both handguns aimed at her while Max stood in front of her with a blank expression. Kye's eyes must have looked wild because Barret turned one gun to aim at him, and it was then Kye realized he'd drawn his own weapon.

"Put that gun away, son," Max said to Kye in his snakelike calm. "I was just explaining to Miss Granville her options; perhaps you'd be so kind as to reiterate for me."

"Kye," Eliana said in a pleading voice as she barely managed to look at him. Her face was red and eyes were leaking tears. The way her arm was pinned behind her back was dangerously close to dislocating her shoulder, and he could tell she was in extreme pain. "Kye!" she begged again.

"Do what he says, Eli," Kye said, holstering his gun. While Eliana may have been pinned to the desk, they were both backed into a corner and at this moment, Eliana needed Kye to be the rock. If he lost his cool, he'd lose his position with Max, and it was likely the favor he garnered with the Senior Demon that was keeping her alive.

"Sound advice, Miss Granville," Max agreed and placed a hand on Kye's shoulder. "Your friend here is trying to keep you alive; I'd listen to him if I were you."

Eliana let out a short sob as she struggled to keep her feet under her. The least movement sent white-hot pain through her shoulder and back to the point she could hardly breathe. What hurt more than that was the vacant expression on Kye's face. She had expected him to come barreling in, shoot these assholes and be done with it. Instead, he was siding with them! It was enough to break her.

"Alright."

"What was that?" Max asked coyly.

"Alright!" Eliana yelled. "I'll do it!"

"Very good, Miss Granville," Max said, and the moment he did the enforcer at her back released her arm. Eliana collapsed to the floor, and her hand immediately flew to her sore shoulder. Kye moved forward to help her up, but she pushed him away much to Max's amusement. "Now, now, I'd hate to be the cause of a lover's quarrel. Don't be too hard on the kid, Miss Granville. Kye is my most loyal soldier." Max moved back to his desk and took a seat in the chair. Opening the top drawer to light another cigar, he gathered the papers and handed them to Eliana who snatched them away.

"We're not lovers," she argued. Turning her scathing glare back to Kye, she sent every ounce of hatred and anger into him that she felt in that moment. "We're not even friends."

"Well, see now, that's too bad," Max cooed and snapped his fingers. The two enforcers began cleaning up the mess on the desk and gathering the boxes of case evidence from the floor to take outside. "You may not know this, but Kye has kept his eye on you all these years." Both Eliana and Kye looked back at Max. "Oh sure, he made what… six trips down to Cambridge to see you?"

"Kye never came to visit me," Eliana said in confusion, but when she looked back at Kye, he had a guilty expression.

"No?" Max asked, but clearly he already knew the answer. "Didn't you know he was the anonymous benefactor of the All Saint's Scholarship you were awarded four years in a row?" Eliana's small gasp echoed her shock as she looked at Kye for the truth of it. His inability to hold her gaze was all the answer she needed.

"I'm going to be sick," Eliana said and felt so light-headed she had to lean over Max's desk.

"Oh dear, we've exhausted our new lawyer. Kye, be a good sport and take Miss Granville home."

"Home?" she asked, thinking of her house back in New Hampshire.

"Max…" Kye said as equal parts warning and request.

"Now," was all Max said with a wave of his hand. Kye knew exactly what Max meant, and he also knew this was likely to tear Eliana apart. He gently wrapped an arm around her shoulders and began leading her out of the room. "I expect a full update in one week, Miss Granville."

Neither of them replied, and Kye sent one last look

back at Max who was grinning like a cat who'd caught the canary. This man was pure evil. The two enforcers followed them outside and back to Kye's car where they loaded the two cardboard boxes of casework into the trunk. Kye helped Eliana into the passenger side of the car, and she didn't look at him once as he retraced their route back down Hell Hollow Road and into town.

Eliana was past the point of tears and was firmly rooted into a level of anger she didn't know she possessed. Had her entire life been one big lie? What made matters worse was that her father was no longer around to scream at. She was so angry she didn't even notice the familiarity of the roads until they were pulling into a driveway.

"Eli," Kye said softly, and she let out a bitter laugh that bordered on hysterical as she observed her childhood home. Kye reached for her hand, but she ignored it as she exited the car and slammed the door. She nearly ripped the back door off the hinge as she yanked it open and retrieved her suitcase. Kye quickly followed as she was stomping toward the front door.

"If this doesn't ice the fucking cake," she muttered. Obviously, Max would house her here. In this ninth circle of hell reserved for treachery and betrayal, the new catchphrases of her life. Was she really ready to reenter the home that had housed the worst years of her life? Turning the knob to pull the front door open, she was met with a latched lock. Tugging on it angrily, she screamed in frustration when it wouldn't open.

"Here," Kye offered as he used one of the keys on his keychain. It slid easily into the lock and turned. With a click, it unlatched the bolt, and he opened the door for her to enter first. Eliana shoved her way inside and slammed her suitcase on the floor of the foyer. How many times had she found her dad passed out just inside this doorway?

When Kye flicked the light on, Eliana was surprised to see the house was almost completely renovated. New hardwood floors, fresh paint on the walls instead of old wallpaper. The living room to her right was redecorated with expensive furniture and what smelled to be freshly steam-cleaned carpet. The fireplace had been gutted and replaced with a gas-powered one that Kye turned on with a remote.

The walls that had previously been bare were now lined with decorative paintings and photographs. There was even wax fruit in a bowl on the coffee table. Eliana felt like a stranger in her home.

"Who lives here?" Eliana asked and felt her skin crawling with discomfort. Everything felt so entirely wrong.

"No one, really," Kye said, standing next to the fire-place. He'd hoped it would cast a homier ambiance for her. "We own a lot of houses in town. It keeps things in the family. Max likes to control who moves in and out of town."

"So you had nothing to do with this?" she asked, glaring at him. Kye looked away. Eliana scoffed and crossed her arms as she moved toward the kitchen. The front door opened again as the enforcers from before entered and set the boxes on the dining room table between matching silver candlesticks and under the new chandelier.

The one who had been pinning Eliana against the desk whispered something to Kye, and Eliana watched nervously as both of their eyes turned to her. What payment was she required to offer now? Kye shook his head and said something to the enforcer who nodded before handing Kye something. Eliana felt momentarily relieved as the two of them left, and Kye locked the door behind them. He walked slowly toward her, and she held her ground near the table as he approached. Holding his hand out to show her what he'd been given, Eliana felt outrage well up in her again.

"Wrist or ankle?" he asked with a hard swallow. In his hand, he held what Eliana recognized as a house-arrest bracelet that was already lit with a red blinking light.

"You're joking," she said coldly. "I'm not wearing that."

"Max thinks you're a flight risk."

"I am."

"You can't run, Eli," Kye protested.

"Are you going to shoot me?" she asked with hands on her hips. "Go ahead, Kye, shoot me. I'd rather it be you than one of Max's goombas out there!"

"I'm not going to shoot you, but you do have to wear this."

"No."

"Yes."

"No!"

Kye growled in frustration and grabbed her wrist to slide it on. She yanked her hand away and when he reached for her again, she slapped him. Kye stared at her for a moment, his temper rising. He grabbed Eliana and pushed her on to the dining room table, the candlesticks clattering to the floor, before dropping to slide the monitor onto her ankle but before he could, she slid off and started walking away from him in indignation.

"Ow!" she yelled when he grabbed her arm and yanked her backward, and she bumped into his chest. Shoving him hard enough for him to step backward, she slapped him again. Kye's jaw clenched. He'd been hit in the face one too many times today.

Eliana cried out as Kye slammed her into the wall, the picture next to her crashing to the ground, the wood frame splintering. When he took her wrist, forcing the bracelet on, she immediately pulled it off and threw it across the room.

"Damnit!" Kye yelled and took her by the neck to hold her against the wall. His grip was tight enough to hold her in place, but not enough to choke her, and she dared him with her eyes to try. His nostrils were flaring as he struggled to keep his temper in check. The fire in her eyes was smoldering, and Kye felt a sudden surge of desire so strong he didn't even try to quell it.

Moving his hand from her throat to the back of her neck, he jerked her so her face was forced to look up at his at a painful angle. Eliana likewise returned the aggression and took fistfuls of his shirt. Her jaw was clenched, and her breathing was coming out in short, angry rasps. She didn't know whether to bite until she tasted blood or knee him in the groin. Instead, she reached for his gun that was holstered behind his back.

He beat her to the grab and twisted her arm behind her back, her chest pressing up against him as he held her in place. Though it was the same arm from before, his grip was hardly as painful. When Eliana realized how much restraint his grip on her had by not snapping her arm in half the way she knew he could, she comprehended the heaves in his chest weren't just from rage but desire. Her eyes searched his, the heat between them ignited, and she tugged her handful of his shirt hard enough to bring his lips down to hers.

4

ye had her up against the wall again in a flash and used the leverage to hoist her up, her legs wrapping instantly around his torso. Her knees dug into his sides in blissful pain, and he used his hip bones to pin her more firmly against the wall. Shamelessly grinding her hips into him, Kye compounded her lust by claiming her mouth with his tongue and pulling hard at the roots of her hair. Eliana's fingernails dug into the back of his neck, heat pulsing between her legs as she bucked against him. The fine line between fury and passion had lit up like a fuse that sent waves of explosive desire through them like wild-fire through tissue paper.

Eliana yanked his jacket off one arm at a time, and holding her by the backside, he turned her around to drop her hard onto the dining table. She yelped against his mouth when Kye's nails scratched her chest as he tore her shirt open. Still wearing the pastel yellow bra with lace he'd seen her in just that morning, his mouth dropped from her mouth to her chest. His teeth grazed her soft flesh, and Eliana cried out again when he bit a nipple through the fabric.

Her knees were gripping him agonizingly as he forced her farther onto the table to lean over her. Kye practically ripped her blouse off and showed the same courtesy to her bra as he tore at the hooks so hard they bent. Once her breasts were free, he reclaimed the sore nipple, this time sucking it into his hot mouth. Her moans echoed through him, and his erection was throbbing painfully in his jeans.

Eliana's eyes closed, feeling every frantic rush of erotic sensation Kye was giving her. She could feel herself pulsing, desperate for him to give her some relief. She dug her fingers into his hair and lifted her hips, signaling exactly where she wanted him to go. Kye kissed from her breasts down her stomach, and his hand cupped her between the legs.

"Kye," she breathed and ground her hips against him, her sensitive places begging for attention. He was kissing her again, her hands clawing up his back. The feel of every firm muscle moving beneath her fingers was like gripping lightning. Eliana couldn't help her sharp inhalation when his erection tucked between her legs, and he ground against her. Her jeans rubbed her heat enough to send a quick pulse of pleasure. One that demanded another one.

Sucking his lower lip between her teeth, she nibbled at his soft mouth and slowly started rocking her hips against his length. Like she had moments before, Kye let out a long moan of pleasure and yearning. Her pelvis was rubbing his length, and his body jerked involuntarily. Eliana ached with the need to be filled, and Kye was gloriously envisioning himself sliding inside her tight, wet places. His mind went blank when her hand tucked between them, and she began stroking him over his pants.

"Eli," he struggled to say, and he felt himself rubbing against her. She didn't reply but began fiddling with his belt as she struggled to unhook it. "Eli, don't," he protested unconvincingly. When she managed to get it undone and her hand slid down the top of his pants, he flung himself off her as though she'd scalded him.

"What is it?" she snapped and sat up. Kye was still backing away. His shirt was creased and stretched from where she'd pulled at him, and she could clearly see his rock-hard member bulging through his jeans.

"I'm not going to fuck you on the dining room table," he said, taking several deep breaths to try to slow his heart rate.

"Why not?" she asked, looking around in confusion.

Her body was craving release, and the fact that he was depriving her of it made her agitated.

"Because it's not right," Kye replied, raking a hand through his hair that had come loose from the ponytail. He looked up at Eliana who was sitting on the edge of the table, hair a mess, eyeliner smeared, bare breasts rising and falling with every breath.

"So let's go upstairs," she offered and slid to the floor. She stepped up against him and rose on her toes to kiss him, but he turned his head, not trusting himself to touch her again. Eliana stepped back in shock and scoffed at him as he rejected her. "You're an asshole," she snapped. Grabbing her shredded blouse and bra she held it over her chest, her cheeks burning with embarrassment. "Was what Max said about the scholarship true?" she asked, still trying to gather herself.

"Eli…"

"Was it?" she asked again in a louder voice. Kye only nodded. Eliana was fuming again. She walked up to him, jaw set and eyes narrowed. "Don't think this means I owe you a damn thing," she snarled and left the room. Kye heard her stomp up the stairs and a door slam. He groaned as he stuffed his hand down his pants to adjust his position to one that was slightly less painful. Maybe he should have fucked her on the table.

ELIANA WAS LAYING on her side when the alarm on her phone chirped the next morning. The sun was just cresting the horizon, but there was enough light to fill the room. When she was a teenager, she'd always loved that her room was eastern facing because the morning light was a cheerful wake-up call, but at this moment Eliana completely hated it.

Her room had remained relatively untouched over the years. Whether that was a good thing or not, she didn't know. They'd had to leave town with no notice so there were still a few trinkets on her dresser she hadn't seen in years. The same bathrobe hung on the back of the door, and her end table still housed her old books. The only new addition was the bedding.

Her old comforter was a bright pink and white with matching striped sheets, but this new one was all white with blue sheets that matched the new paint on her walls. The old photographs she'd pinned to the walls and the magazine clippings of lawyers, Harvard memorabilia, and inspirational quotes she'd hung to keep her motivated in school were replaced with generic, hotel looking artwork.

The night before she hadn't so much as turned the light on to examine anything. She'd faced enough ghosts in one day. Now that the sun was rising she couldn't ignore the time-capsule she'd slept in. While the rest of the house looked renovated, re-carpeted and painted, this room had been touched up, but she could still see the pink stain under her desk where she'd spilled a bottle of nail polish when she was ten.

Eliana groaned as she rolled onto her back. Her body was tense from the lack of gratification the night before. Letting out an angry sigh, she berated herself for how easily she'd given in to Kye. She'd bucked and pawed and opened her legs for him like a horny teenager. But hadn't he wanted her too? Or was he just a guy responding to a pathetically desperate and topless woman?

Shivering, Eliana remembered how he'd felt. Despite her sense of humiliation at how he'd ultimately rejected her, she couldn't deny how if it were up to her, she would have stripped him naked and rode him like a mechanical bull right there on the dining room table. There was something so primal in the way she desired him. Ten years of pent-up sexual tension did that to a girl. Hadn't Eliana had the same cravings for him in high school after their first kiss? Hell, the first time he'd seen her topless was in this very room.

I guess not much has changed, she mused as she swung her legs out of bed. She froze when she looked down at her bare legs and saw the black apparatus around her ankle. Tugging at it, the monitor was secured in place and the red light was blinking exactly every five seconds. Kye had obviously snuck in her room after she'd fallen asleep and slid it on.

Her indignation rose faster than a fat man's blood pressure, and she growled as she slammed her suitcase open and dressed. Her yellow bra was destroyed, so she opted for a cream bando under a white v-neck blouse. She spent twenty minutes and burned a few hundred calories trying to get her black skinny jeans over the ankle monitor. Her loud cursing must have alerted someone in the house because she could hear movement downstairs before she finished brushing her hair, freshening her face, and leaving the room.

Eliana could smell coffee brewing even before she got downstairs, and when she entered the kitchen, her eyes immediately landed on the dining room table. Her cheeks turned pink when she saw Kye stooped on the ground sweeping up the broken picture they'd knocked off the wall only hours before.

"Hi," he said shortly as he stood up with a dustpan in one hand and a broom in the other. Eliana stared blankly at him before turning away and moving to a cabinet to retrieve a mug. She was pouring a cup from the practically brand-new coffee maker when Kye emptied the pan into the garbage under the sink and stood next to her. She made to turn away from him when he gently placed a hand on her arm.

"Yes?" she asked harshly as she looked from his hand

to his eyes. He'd obviously showered that morning because his hair was still wet, and he smelled of soap.

"Don't be mad," he requested, and Eliana rolled her eyes.

"Why would I be mad?" she asked sarcastically as she set her cup down and placed her hands on her hips. "Why would I be mad, Kye?" she asked again, and he braced for the impending lecture. "Oh, you mean mad because my entire life has been a lie? Mad because when I thought I was finally escaping this town, I find out my entire adult life has been funded by the people who have been wanting to kill me? Mad because I got wrapped up in a sick crime lord's twisted game, through no fault of my own, and now I have to work off a debt I never personally incurred? Mad because my childhood sweetheart lied to me for the last ten years? Mad because rather than earning a scholarship on my own merit, I was actually the product of a scheme to ensure my law degree could be used to advance a criminal organization that said sweetheart practically runs? Or mad because despite all that, like a pathetic moron, I threw myself at him and actually asked him to fuck me on the dining room table of my childhood home that's been commandeered for the use of a motorcycle club? Mad? I'm not mad. I'm insane," she concluded, and Kye rubbed the back of his neck as he looked down at her.

"It's not as bad as all that," he tried to console. Eliana

scoffed again, and when she turned away from him, he wrapped an arm around her midsection. She tried to pull away from him, but his grip was too tight. "You're not a moron," Kye said gently in her ear, and she stilled. Taking the cue, he slowly turned her around to face him. Her expression was unreadable, but she was clearly listening to him. "Eli, it's not that I didn't want you or that I don't want you," he corrected, "but I'm not going to have you like some hookup. I promised you once that if we were going to be together, I'd do it right. Make it special. I'm not going back on that now."

"That's not up to you, Kye," Eliana said, backing up. "You don't get to decide the wheres, whens, and hows of every detail in my life. If you want me, then you can either have me as I am or not at all. I'm not some dainty princess who wants to be coddled on a bed of rose petals," she said with a wave of her hand. "You don't get to decide what makes something special. In fact, from here on out, you don't get to decide anything for me ever again."

"I'm sorry," he said, stuffing his hands in his pockets. "I'm sorry you feel lied to and that you're caught in this. I get it if you don't believe me, but I was trying to shelter you from this. I've been climbing the ranks, waiting for Max to be out, in order to suspend the contract on you and your dad. I never forgot about you or what you meant to me… what you still mean to me."

"You've got a funny way of showing it," Eliana muttered and took up her mug again before sipping the black liquid. The brief silence was interrupted when her phone chimed.

"What was that?" Kye asked, and Eliana pulled the device from her back pocket. "Give me that!" Kye said as he snatched it from her hand.

"Kye!" she protested and reached for it. "What do you think I'm going to do? Call the police? My guess is, Max owns every cop in this town."

"You're not wrong," Kye admitted. "We've had county sheriffs on the payroll for six years now…"

"Exactly," Eliana continued. "In the meantime, I still have a job back home. One that was expecting me in the office an hour ago. Now, either you let me call in and tell them I'm going to cash in my bereavement leave and likely vacation time, or my boss is going to know I'm missing. Want to know how fast a law firm of nosy and concerned lawyers can track someone down?" Eliana held her hand out expectantly. Kye hesitated before handing it back to her.

"Fine, but no one else. Don't bring anyone else into this, for their sake as well as yours," Kye cautioned. Eliana took the phone and quickly punched in a text to her boss, Jason Nelson of Nelson, Watford, and Shier. Knowing the older man was very fond of her, she didn't anticipate any problems taking the time off; although she wouldn't have minded if he sent the troops out looking for her. "What now?" Kye asked as she tucked the phone into her pocket and sat at the table.

"Now," Eliana began as she set her mug down and began pulling the first box in front of her, "you're going to make breakfast and I'm going to get to work. The sooner I do, the sooner this nightmare is over, right?"

"Right," Kye agreed, and he opened the refrigerator at the same time she opened the lid to the box.

5

Despite the warmer weather, Kye was reclining in the living room in the armchair in front of the lit fireplace. Grier was across from him, beer in hand, feet propped on the coffee table. He'd arrived the day before to help with "babysitting" as he'd called it. It was late afternoon, and the two of them were chatting quietly. His eyes wandered across the foyer to where he could see Eliana at the dining room table.

She was on the phone, clearly pleading with the person on the other line, as she waved a piece of paper in the air. He could only make out every other word of her rant before she dropped the phone to the table. The other person must have hung up on her. In the last five days, she'd barely left that table.

The boxes had long since been emptied of the paperwork and were now piled in some sort of organized mess that only Eliana could understand. From what he'd observed of her, she was incredible. Sifting through every piece of evidence that had been stacked against the two men, she insisted on working the case from the reverse.

If I can prosecute them, I can defend them, she'd said in a half daze at three in the morning a few days ago. Even though he didn't have the faintest idea on how to be a lawyer, he knew what odds were, and they were definitely stacked against them.

Eli Torrez and Brock Crawford had not only been spotted at the bar in Portland, but video surveillance had them entering the back alley at eleven thirty, ten minutes before reports of gunfire were called in, and the same camera showed them fleeing the scene before they were hauled in by police an hour later. Their guns, which had clearly been fired recently, were still on them.

"I say those bastards are getting what they deserve," Grier commented as he swigged the last of his beer. "Torrez and Crawford were real bastards."

"That's no secret," Kye agreed. He was still watching Eliana. She was rubbing her neck as though it ached, and she stood to pour herself another cup of coffee. That woman caffeinated like a junky.

"Think she can do it?" Grier asked as he reached over the table to check the contents of Kye's beer. Seeing it was empty, he frowned.

"I don't know," Kye admitted.

"You'd better have a backup plan if she can't," Grier suggested, and Kye looked at him with a raised eyebrow. "I know you, Kye," he said, "if Eliana can't get these guys off death row, you're not going to let Max kill her. You've been in love with her for years."

"You're right, I won't let him kill her," Kye agreed. Grier stood and picked up both empty bottles.

"What are you going to do?"

"I don't know," Kye said with a shrug. Grier nodded and made his way into the kitchen where he tossed the bottles into the sink and opened the fridge to fetch more. He popped the lid to one and took a swig as he looked over at Eliana who was leaning over the edge of the table reading a dissertation. The front of her blouse was coming down ever so slightly, and Grier glanced at Kye who was texting on his phone, before returning his eyes to the supple skin he could just see the tops of.

Feeling eyes on her, Eliana looked up to see Grier staring at her chest, and she quickly stood upright. Her eyes narrowed at him, and Grier shrugged as he'd been caught. "Want one?" he asked, referring to the beer in his hand. Eliana adjusted her glasses, pursed her lips, and didn't bother responding as she went back to work. Opening a second one, he walked over and set it in front of her. "My contribution to the war effort," he teased.

"Thanks," Eliana said sarcastically as she moved it off

the stack of papers he'd set it on. The condensation from the outside had left a ring on the paper. Sighing in frustration, she picked it up and began shaking it to dry the water.

"You understand all this?" Grier asked, picking up a paper and reading over it. "It's not even English…"

"No," Eliana corrected and pulled the paper out of his hand, "some of it is Latin."

"Latin?"

"Yes, Latin."

"Who speaks Latin?" Grier asked, leaning on the table.

"Lawyers and doctors," Eliana replied shortly. "It's a dead language. You know, dead? Like I'm going to be if I don't have this done in the next two days." Her short tone was an indication she wanted him to leave her alone. Grier wasn't catching the hint.

"Kye won't let Max kill you," Grier said, picking at the label on his bottle. "He's still in love with you."

"He's got a funny way of showing it," Eliana stated, still distracted by something she was reading.

"If Max would do us all a favor and die, we could get this mess taken care of a lot easier," Grier commented, and Eliana looked up from the stack.

"If so many people want him dead, why doesn't someone just kill him?" she asked only half sarcastically.

"Not the way it works," Grier said, turning around to

face her more fully. "Max gets offed, it'd be anarchy. Every officer would claim a bid for his throne. It'd be like the incident with the Defectors times a hundred. The whole club would collapse if Max didn't appoint a predecessor."

"You say that like it's a bad thing," Eliana said, standing upright. She surpassed her coffee and grabbed the beer he'd brought her. Lifting his bottle in a small salute, they both drank.

"It may not be bad for you, but it'd be bad for a lot of people. The Screaming Demons are the main source of income and jobs in this town. You might live, but a lot of others would lose their livelihood."

"Livelihood that's supported by crime? I don't feel bad about that," she said, removing her glasses and tossing them on to the table.

"For a lawyer, you're pretty ignorant."

"Excuse me?"

"You talk like everything is black and white, and it's not."

"The law is pretty clear…"

"The law is open to interpretation; that's how you have a job," Grier interrupted. "Not everything is right or wrong. There can be a wrong way to do the right thing and a right way to do the wrong thing. We live in a world of gray areas. Sooner you see that the better off you'll be."

"Like these two murdering that man in an alley?" Eliana asked, holding up the file with the mugshots.

"Maybe he had it coming," Grier offered.

"Maybe he did, but what about the seven people caught in the crossfire during the police shootout? Three of them died, one is paralyzed, and one of them is brain dead. Did they have it coming?"

"Probably not," Grier said, shrugging again. "The cops shot too. Their bullets do damage just like anyone else's."

"You'll find a reason to justify anything with that attitude," Eliana argued, and Grier smiled.

"Exactly, it's how I manage to walk through life guilt-free." Sighing in frustration, she looked away from him. She wasn't going to argue morality with someone who clearly didn't have a conscience.

"Any progress?" Kye asked as he entered the room. Eliana placed her hands on her hips, eyes narrowed.

"No," she said shortly. He could still feel her anger. She'd been wearing it like a second skin since she'd arrived. Keeping her sentences short and sure to never stand within his arm's reach, she was seething with contempt. "I can't think in here anymore," she complained, running a hand through her hair. "If I'm going to find anything, it isn't in here," she said, gesturing to the paperwork. "I need to go to the crime scene."

"In Portland?"

"It's only two hours away," she defended. "Is my prison bracelet going to electrocute me if we go for a drive?"

"I'll make a call," Kye said and grabbed his cut off the back of the chair he'd draped it on.

"I can drive you two," Grier offered and downed the rest of his beer.

"No thanks," Eliana said, reaching for her coat. "I'm trying to get two people off for murder; I'm not up for defending a DUI while I'm at it." Kye laughed, and Grier glared at her as the two exited the house through the front door. Tossing his bottle angrily into the kitchen, it shattered against the cabinet, and he cursed.

* * *

"WHAT ARE WE LOOKING FOR?" Kye asked as he sat on the hood of his car and watched Eliana pacing the alley between brick buildings. She'd been mostly silent the entire car ride, and he was struggling to find a way to get her to talk. He could tell her mind was singularly focused on the case, and he couldn't blame her. Any way they painted the picture, someone's life was in danger.

"I don't know," Eliana admitted as she came to a stop next to one of the dumpsters. She was comparing the alley with a photograph of the crime scene in her hand.

"I've got an airtight case why these men are guilty and no way to refute the evidence."

"You'll find something," Kye encouraged as he lit a cigarette. He saw Eliana's posture go rigid, and she dropped her arms to her sides. "What is it?"

"I won't, Kye," she said so quietly he almost didn't hear her. "I'm not going to find what isn't here," she said, turning slowly to face him. Her eyes were filling with tears, and he pushed himself off his car to walk toward her.

"Hey, come on, we'll think of something."

"There isn't anything, don't you get it?" she asked angrily. "I've been handed an airtight case. These two have exhausted all of their appeals, been sentenced twice, and have spent the last thirteen months on death row. The taxpayers aren't going to fund any more trials. The district attorney personally oversaw this case. Two officers were killed during the shootout. People are out for blood. At best, I can petition the mayor for a stay-of-execution, but without any new evidence, they don't stand a chance of even being considered for a lesser sentence let alone having the charges dropped."

"Can we refute any of the evidence?" Kye asked.

"There's testimony from ten witnesses that these men were causing a scene in the bar and got into a verbal and physical altercation with the victim before they chased him into the alley and shot him. Then, rather than surrendering when they were caught, they engaged in a shootout in a public location. The list of charges is longer than the city census. I'm fucked!" Eliana yelled and threw the papers in her hands.

"Come here," Kye said, taking her by the shoulders and pulling her into a hug. She didn't return the gesture, but she didn't pull away either.

"He's going to kill me," Eliana choked out, and Kye gripped her tighter.

"You let me worry about Max," Kye said, and his mind was already churning, trying to think of anything that might help.

"Let's just go," Eliana said, pulling back to look up at him. "Let's get in the car and drive away."

"I doubt that would work," Kye told her. "Max would hunt both of us down and kill us. He's got a thing about loyalty."

"Oh, he's got a thing for loyalty," Eliana said with a bitter laugh and backed away from him.

"What's that supposed to mean?"

"We could do it, Kye. We could get in your car and drive to the border and never look back, but you're scared."

"I'm scared?"

"Yes, you're terrified. I can see it on your face," she said, dismissing him with a hand.

"What am I supposed to be scared of?" he asked, crossing his arms.

"You're terrified to lose your status," Eliana replied. "You've built yourself a little kingdom up here in Maine with your biker buddies and your club, and you don't want to lose it."

"You have no idea what you're talking about," he scoffed.

"Oh, don't I?" she retorted. "This is exactly the way it was before when we were in high school. You'd found a modicum of approval from Max, and you didn't want to give that up for anyone or anything. You'd make some grand statement that you were doing it for me, for us, for love, but it was all bullshit! You were doing it for yourself. Harboring some underlying daddy issue, you wanted this life. You needed this life."

"So you've got it all figured out," Kye said, challenging her with his height. "Poor, lost, pathetic little foster nobody Kye really just wanted a place to belong, is that it?"

"You had a place you belonged," Eliana countered, not backing down from him. "You belonged with me. I begged you to come away with me. I had everything we needed, but it wasn't enough for you. I wasn't enough for you."

"You're wrong, you're so wrong," he spat. "I wasn't going to move into your college apartment like some charity case. Following you around while you made something of your life. And in case you forgot, that life was still financed by Max's stolen merchandise."

"Make all the excuses you want, Kye, you're scared of trying to make it on your own. You've set all your ambitions on taking over the Screaming Demons, and nothing will deter you from that. God knows, I'm going to meet with Max in two days, and he'll probably tell you to shoot me yourself. And you know what, I bet you'll do it. I bet you'll use that gun tucked behind your back to blow my brains out, and then you'll mop the floor for him."

"You're stupid if you think that's true. I've been the one keeping you safe all these years. If you hadn't made it through law school, do you think Max would have waited this long to keep his hands off you? He would have hauled you and your dad in years ago and killed you."

"Then or now, what's the difference," Eliana said, shaking her head. "Either way, in two days I'm dead. I can't win this case. Maybe I just don't care anymore…"

"What did you say?" Kye asked, his brows furrowing.

"I've lost everything, Kye," she stated. "There's no going back from this, and we both know it. Either I'm dead in two days or I spend the rest of my life working for Max. He's not the kind of guy to just forgive a debt, and you know it. My whole life has been a lie. I'm never going to get back to my life in New Hampshire, and the man I was in love with won't get in that car with me and drive away. What's the point?" There was a resignation to her voice that shook Kye to the core.

"Where are you going?" he asked as she sulked past the car toward the entrance to the alley. She stopped and pointed to her left.

"I'm going into that bar to get drunk," she stated. "Either come with or kill me now." When Kye didn't move at first, she laughed bitterly and held both arms out to make his kill shot easier. Kye sighed and pressed the lock button on his car.

"I'll buy."

6

$\mathcal{E}$liana couldn't help fidgeting with the hem of her pink shirt as she once again found herself in the all-white office standing before the man who held her life in the palm of his hand. Not unlike the stone hand that held a bird just behind her. The same two men stood at the door as before, but this time Kye was next to her. Though his presence offered her some comfort, she was still barely a step above terrified when Max looked up at her. He was obviously displeased.

"I must say I'm disappointed, Miss Granville," Max said, closing the paperwork. "I give you five days and this is the best you can do? The chance of a technicality?"

"There's a massive flaw in that logic," Eliana defended. "A team of prosecutors had six months to build a case, and you give me five days with no access to a team or original evidence bags, and you expect me to debunk a DA. I didn't take you for a religious man, Mr. Strong. What you're asking for would be nothing short of an act of God."

"What I expect, Miss Granville, is that when I give an order it is carried out," Max said, slamming a hand on the desk. The sound made Eliana jump but she stuck to her guns.

"I've done that," she declared. "The victim, Hugo Mortise, was not only shot, he was stabbed. Only the gun was found. If we can submit a subpoena for the autopsy and have an independent coroner determine the cause of death was a stabbing and not a bullet wound, then we have the new evidence required to go back to trial."

"Suppose the petition is denied."

"Suppose it's accepted," she countered.

"That doesn't take care of the charges that ensued during the shootout. It was the death of those two badges that earned them the chair. What do you propose we do about that?" His voice was full of agitation, and the oxygen tank he was breathing from was working overtime the way he was huffing and puffing.

"If we can get a retrial, then we use the witness statements to create a reasonable doubt that Torrez and Crawford shot first."

"Self-defense against the police?" Max asked indignantly. "That's a long shot."

"Torrez is Hispanic, Crawford's mom was full blood Inuit. If we play the racial profiling card, the jury will squirm. It's a hot topic these days, and they won't shy away from a hate crime by armed officers, who according to their profiles, are all white."

"If, if, if, that's all I'm hearing are 'ifs'," Max snapped and yanked the tube from his nose. "Do you or do you not have a solid case for me?" Eliana glanced at Kye who kept his stoic gaze forward. With a shaky sigh, Eliana shook her head no. Max made a gesturing motion to the two men at the door, and one of them opened it.

Kye visibly tensed when Dhal walked in. Their bad blood was still bubbling under the surface. What made Eliana visibly pale was the gun he wore on his right hip. Dhal walked forward, his shoulder slamming into Kye's as he did.

"It seems Miss Granville is unable to fulfill her end of the bargain," Max said coolly as he walked around to the other side of his desk to stand in front of Dhal. "I think you know what needs to be done." Eliana looked worryingly at Kye who remained infuriatingly placid, even when Dhal began reaching for his side. She stepped backward when Dhal turned toward her, but instead of the gun from his holster, he held his cell phone.

From his position, barely an arm's length away, she

could hear the phone ringing from the other end. "Steward?" he asked when the other person picked up. "It's done, light it up." There was muttering on the other end of the phone, and Dhal hung up. He slid his phone back into his pocket, looked Eliana up and down once more, and brushed past them as he left.

"That's it?" Eliana asked when the room fell silent. Max was sitting on the edge of his desk with arms folded.

"What did you expect? An execution?" There was a tension in his voice she guessed was either aggravation or condescension. "In case you hadn't noticed, I have a particular way I like to keep my office," he said, stepping toward her. "It wouldn't do to have your brains splattered all over my clean carpet." Max lifted a hand to brush her cheek, and she flinched.

"Then what..." Her question was cut short when Max backhanded her. The hit knocked her head to the side, but her shock made her eyes fly back to his. Seeing it as defiance, Max drew his arm back and punched her straight in the mouth. With a short cry, the blow sent her to the floor and before she could gather herself, he used his foot to shove her onto her back and pinned her by the throat. Eliana choked on the pressure and tried to push his foot off, but that only made him press down harder. Her vision began to swim, and her eyes frantically looked to Kye.

"Max," Kye said with pleading in his voice, and his hand twitched toward his own gun.

"Don't cross me, boy. You'd be dead before you chambered a bullet," Max warned, pointing at him. From the door, both enforcers had their automatic weapons drawn on him. Eliana felt near passing out, her legs kicking wildly as she tried to free herself. "Besides, I've decided to give her another chance," Max said and removed his foot. Gasping for air, her hand flew to her neck. Eliana rolled onto her side and feared she may vomit.

"Don't touch me," she rasped out when Kye tried to help her up. Max laughed as he watched the interaction.

"Don't be too mad at the boy," Max said, sitting on the edge of his desk again. "It's him you have to thank for me not wringing that pretty neck of yours." Eliana looked at Max in confusion, her hand still clutching her throat. "He told me all about your assessment of the situation. Having a high-profile case so closely linked to the club would not serve our best interests."

"So you never wanted me to get them acquitted?" she asked, and her throat hurt terribly when she tried to talk. "Was this all part of your sick game?"

"Don't test me, Miss Granville," Max warned. "I wanted Torrez and Crawford free, but those two jack-asses had to get themselves caught on camera and tried to shoot their way out. If there's no way to get the charges dismissed completely, they've secured their own fate. As I told you before, I won't have them tied to our organization."

"If you leave them in prison, what's going to stop them from talking?" Eliana asked as she felt her vision finally restored. "If they have dirt on you, the DA will offer them a deal."

"Oh, they've already been offered a deal," Max stated and bit down on the cigar that had previously been smoldering from the ashtray on his desk. "But don't you worry, they won't last the night," he said, blowing out a puff of smoke. "There's going to be a fight in their cell block. Poor guys won't make it."

"You'll kill your men, just like that?" she asked in morbid shock.

"A better question to ask is, 'if I'm willing to kill my own men, what will I be willing to do to you if you let me down again'. That's a question you'd better spend the next forty-eight hours thinking very carefully on," Max advised. "I've got nearly a dozen guys sitting in county cells I want to be released. I'll get you the information, you get it done."

"That's my second chance?" Eliana asked.

"No, that's what you're going to do while I consider keeping you on the payroll or killing you," he answered, pointing at her with his cigar. "It couldn't hurt your case to get them released. Even better if you get state patrol off my back."

"So that's it? I stay caught in the web of your agenda? I free a dozen men and you'll, what, let me go? Send me home? Why don't I believe that?" she asked with a wave of nausea crashing into her. Max approached her once again, and she visibly cringed when he trailed a finger along the red mark on her throat.

"You're a smart woman," he observed in a low tone. The sickly-sweet smell of his cigar was near as suffocating as his boot. "What did I say about blood on the carpet?" he asked and ran his thumb over her swollen lip where he'd struck her. The blood from her lip covered his thumb, and he licked it off. Eliana nearly gagged. "Get her home," he ordered shortly, and Kye didn't hesitate to take Eliana's arm and pull her from the room.

Kye was quickly pulling her out of the compound and back toward his car when Eliana collapsed. It had rained the night before, and the slick ground and her shaking body contributed to her slip. Kye reached for her, and she shoved him away as she stood.

"This is all your fault!" she screamed and slammed her fists on his chest. "You just stood there! You stood there and did nothing!" Eliana was bordering on hysterical, and she didn't notice the small crowd from the bar watching the interaction. Kye felt powerless to do anything.

"Alright, alright, let's break it up!" Eliana felt a hand on her shoulder and through her tears, she saw Jez standing behind her. She'd been helping to unload the shipping truck of beer crates when she'd seen the interaction. "No need for the theatrics, my girl," she suggested and nodded toward the tough-looking crowd of bikers who were watching them.

"I don't care," she argued and used the back of her hand to wipe her face. The rough action reopened the cut on her lip.

"You will when the guys see you beating up their VP. Whose defense do you think they're going to come to, sweetie?" Eliana only quieted as a response. "KD, get yourself inside and order a round of drinks on the house. I'll take her to get cleaned up."

Feeling she didn't have a say in the matter, like anything else in her life at the present, Eliana followed Jez through the back entrance of the bar, not bothering to look back at Kye who was watching her walk away with desperation in his eyes.

Jez led her straight into what must have been her office and gestured for her to sit. Eliana remained standing as Jez entered the bathroom to fetch something. The office was small. Likely a renovated section of the storage room, but it had a desk, a three-seat couch, a mini-fridge, and two bookshelves. Eliana picked up the framed photo off the desk. It was a younger version of Jez in a hospital bed holding a baby wrapped in a pink blanket.

"You're a nosy one, aren't you?" Jez asked as she reentered the room. In one hand, she had a first aid kit and in the other, she had a black bag that was sealed with a zipper.

"Hazard of being a lawyer," Eliana admitted. Jez once again instructed her to sit, and this time Eliana took a seat on the couch after returning the photo. "Is that your son?"

"Yes," Jez replied shortly as she opened the kit and took out a cotton swab she doused with disinfectant. It stung when she pressed it to the cut on the corner of Eliana's mouth. "He's in Texas with his father," Jez said before Eliana could ask the question. "I haven't seen him since he was four. He'll be sixteen in September."

"Why so long?" Eliana questioned.

"Why do you care?" Jez asked flatly and turned to clean the cut under Eliana's left eye. "Bastard Max always has to wear that damn ring, doesn't he?" she asked rhetorically.

"How did you know Max did this?"

"I've been around a long time, baby girl, cleaned up a lot of faces. You start to recognize a man's handy work. Believe it or not, you're one of the lucky ones."

"What kind of hell hole is this?" Eliana asked, feeling resentment rise in her. If she had the choice, she'd burn the whole place down and roast a marshmallow over the coals.

"The worst kind and don't you forget it," Jez advised. "You wanna know why I haven't seen my son? Because I don't want him anywhere near this place and if that means he is nowhere near me, then so be it."

"Why don't you just leave?" Eliana asked and Jez paused to look her straight in the eye.

"You've no idea what this place really is, do you?" Eliana couldn't answer and Jez chuckled bitterly. "That's good, baby, that means there's hope for you. The less you know the better. Just don't go mistaking Max's restraint for mercy. He likes to toy with his Hell Kats."

"I'm not a…"

"Sure, you are," Jez interrupted. "You may not look the part, but he owns you now. Consider this your brand," she said tapping the cut on her cheek. "So, take my advice, do what he asks, don't talk back and always try to be useful. The second you're not, you disappear." Eliana wanted to ask a million more questions, beg for help even, but her anxiety and dread had overtaken her again. "Now, let me show you how to apply makeup to cover those bruises." Jez unzipped the black bag that held several different shades of concealer for all skin tones. At that moment Eliana knew Jez was right. She'd done this hundreds of times.

"Thank you," she said softly when Jez was finished.

Her face hurt terribly and Eliana was even more grateful when the older woman handed her two pain killers and a shot of vodka to wash it down.

"You're welcome," Jez said sincerely. "Can I give you one more piece of advice?" she asked and Eliana shrugged. "Be nicer to that kid out there."

"Kye? Why?"

"You aren't the only one who's gotten wrapped up in this mess. It's a hell of a lot easier to get pulled in than to climb your way out. That boy would die for the people he loves and something tells me he's got it bad for you."

"Did Ebony tell you that?" Eliana asked sarcastically.

"Jealousy makes any woman look ugly," Jez said, pouring her own glass. "You give him a reason, baby, and he'll take good care of you. KD isn't like the rest of the dogs out there. He's managed to hold on to something good inside. Something pure. Something strong. You give him a reason, and he'll fight for you."

Eliana sat silent for a long moment cradling her glass. When the glass was empty, she handed it back to Jez and slowly made her way back outside where she saw Kye anxiously waiting. "Take me home," she asked softly, and he took her hand in his to lead her away.

7

Kye had opted for his motorcycle instead of the SUV when he'd taken them back to the house. Something in him had needed the release of an adrenaline rush, and the way he tore through town like hell on wheels had given him that. Eliana had clung to him in terror as he'd reached maximum speed on the straight roads. The wind had whipped around her and the spray of water that still lingered on the road sprayed like a muddy shower.

When they reached her old neighborhood, he slowed and pulled his bike to a stop in the driveway. Although still shaken, Eliana was grateful to be back to the familiar location. Her legs had cramped from how firmly she had been gripping them. She noticed the mud splattered on the helmet she wore when she handed it back to Kye. He practically slammed it onto the handlebar of his bike.

Eliana was first inside. The light in the kitchen was still on from earlier, so she headed that direction. The paperwork from the old cases was still littering the table so, with nothing else to occupy her, she began picking them up and shoving them back into boxes. The door slammed startling her and Kye threw his keys onto the kitchen counter. She had every intention of ignoring him but he walked straight up to her and took her by the chin.

"Stop," she protested and pushed his hand away.

"Let me see," he insisted in an agitated tone. She let him hold her chin again while he looked her slightly swollen face over. "Does it hurt?"

"No," she lied and turned away from him. The image of him standing idly by while Max had nearly choked her to death still bothered her.

"You're lying, I'll get you some ice," Kye said and paced to the freezer where he pulled out a white tray. He grabbed the towel from the handle of the oven and began plopping the cubes in the folds.

"Good idea, grab some ice. Put it on your conscience," Eliana suggested. "Hopefully it hurts worse than my face." Kye slammed his fist on the counter and let out two forceful breaths through his nose.

"I didn't know he was going to hit you," Kye said through gritted teeth.

"Now who's lying?" Eliana asked rhetorically as she continued stacking the papers. "You know what Max is like. You knew he was going to retaliate somehow. You said you were going to keep me safe. For all I knew, he was going to kill me!"

"Max doesn't like to personally get his hands dirty," Kye explained. "When I spoke with him, told him the dangers of taking this shit back to trial, I convinced him that you still had value. To give you another chance," Kye defended.

"Another chance?" Eliana asked incredulously. "This wasn't even a first chance!" she yelled and swatted the papers off the table. They blew through the air and Kye let out a long breath as he waited for them to settle.

"You're still alive, both of us are, I call that a win for today."

"Don't expect me to thank you," Eliana muttered and placed both hands on the table. Kye walked over to her and placed a hand on her back.

"I don't," he replied rubbing gentle, soothing circles. His touch calmed her and for the first time in three days, she felt the tremors settle in her body.

"I hate this. I hate feeling trapped."

"I know you do," Kye said empathetically and as she

hadn't pushed him away, he took the chance to pull her closer. "That's how Max gets to you, though. He'll exploit any weakness he can find. Don't let him get into your head. Max isn't showing it, but he's desperate. This last heart attack nearly killed him. I have a feeling I know the players he's trying to get released. Call it a last-ditch-effort, but he's making a final power play trying to ensure his legacy lives on."

"I can't think about this anymore tonight," Eliana said resting her forehead on his shoulder, his hands still attempting to massage the tension out of her muscles. "I just want to close my eyes and pretend we're seventeen again. Does that sound stupid?"

"No, baby," Kye answered grinning down at her. "Close your eyes," he instructed and she smiled as she did. Taking her left hand in his he gently rocked her. He rested his chin on the top of her head and Eliana wrapped her arm around his neck. "We're at prom. Missy just won prom queen, that awful DJ is playing watered down oldies and one of the soccer players just spiked the punch."

"Maybe I'll have a second glass then," Eliana laughed and Kye wrapped her in a tight embrace before releasing her.

"Your wish is my command," he said dramatically and opened the freezer for a second time. Instead of ice, this time he removed a bottle of vodka that frosted over when he set it on the counter. Pouring it into two glasses, they clinked glasses before drinking. "Easy, Tiger," Kye chuckled when she poured herself a second.

"I think I've earned it," she replied and felt the warmth spreading through her abdomen as she drank. "In fact, I think I'm going to take the rest of this upstairs and climb into a hot bath."

"You should eat something," he suggested and Eliana shook her head.

"I'm not hungry, just thirsty," she said sloshing the liquid in the bottle. Kye watched her walk upstairs, the onslaught of alcohol making her hips sway just a little more. A few minutes later he heard the water running upstairs and began pulling contents out of the refrigerator.

* * *

KYE HADN'T HEARD a sound from upstairs in nearly an hour. Tossing his phone onto the counter, he grabbed one of the plates from the table he had set and made his way upstairs. He'd been hoping Eliana would come back down wanting to fill her stomach with more than vodka, so he'd cooked a pot of spaghetti and lit the candlesticks. An hour after the shower had turned off, he lost patience in waiting.

Eliana's door was ajar so he nudged it with his foot, balancing a plate in one hand and a bottle of wine with two glasses in the other. He nearly dropped all of them when he saw Eliana standing at her mirror in nothing but blue lace underwear. She was distracted as she held a book in her hand she was reading and Kye barely managed to duck back out of the room and knock before he was spotted.

"Hold on!" Eliana called and Kye grinned as the image of her plump ass in those panties still filled his mind. "Come in!" Kye entered more loudly this time. She had pulled on an oversized, cotton t-shirt and had slid under the covers of her bed.

"Thought you might have drowned," he joked. "I brought food."

"Mm, I'm starved," Eliana said accepting the plate from him. "Carbs, you read my mind." Giving him a flirty wink she grabbed the fork took a mouthful. "Aren't you eating?" she asked and had to cover her mouth with her hand as it was full of food.

"Mine's downstairs," he said and stepped toward the door.

"Mmm, stay," she protested and caught his hand. "Plenty here for two," she said and offered him the plate back. Kye smiled and kicked the door shut before plopping on the bed next to her and taking the fork.

"What were you reading?" he questioned.

"Huh?" Eliana asked as she tried to pull the wine cork off with her teeth. Kye caught himself, he wasn't supposed to have seen her.

"That," he said recovering quickly as he pointed to the white book on the vanity. "It's still open, figured you were reading it.

"Oh," Eliana said and slid out of bed. Though the shirt was long, it wasn't long enough to deprive him another peek of cheek. "Believe it or not," she began and nearly tripped back into the bed. Kye had to set the plate on the nightstand to keep it from spilling as she dived back under the covers. "This is my old diary," she concluded and flipped through a few pages. "Nothing but Harvard, Harvard, Harvard."

"Oh no!" Kye said and stopped her on a page, "I see my name!" Eliana tugged the book away from him.

"No way, that's private," she said squirming as he reached over her for it.

"Come on what does it say? It's about me I should get to know." He was practically laying on her now and using his long arms he grabbed it from her.

"Kye!" Eliana laughed, "I can't breathe!" he rolled onto his back and held the diary up to read it. Eliana reached for it but he jerked it away.

"Kye Driscoll is so handsome..." he read in an exaggerated tone.

"I never wrote that!" Grabbing it out of his hands she

tossed it into the open closet across the room. Kye tucked an arm behind his head and laughed as Eliana glared down at him.

"You sure?" he asked coyly. Her hair was still damp and small beads of water dripped onto his chest. Eliana shifted so she was laying on her side, head propped up on her arm.

"Maybe once," she admitted and her eyes dropped from his. When he didn't say anything, she looked back up at him and he was grinning with enough ego to thicken the air in the room. "Narcissist," she insulted.

"You say that like it doesn't turn you on," he goaded looking like a lazy cat lounging on the bed. Eliana's eyes dropped again but her arm slowly draped over his abdomen. When he shifted toward her ever so slightly, she sat farther up so she was leaning over him.

"Maybe a little," she said in a lowered tone. Her eyes met his and she ducked her head to kiss him. His free arm wrapped around her back and pulled her against him.

In truth, the page he'd stumbled upon was an entry from the only night they'd had together sleeping in each other's arms. In this very bed. She'd written in explicit detail everything she wished they'd done. Now, with her mind already on that subject, and the very man beneath her, she couldn't hold back.

Kicking free of the covers, she snaked her freshly

shaven leg between his. Her lips were insistent and Kye had to catch his breath when her tongue pushed into his mouth. She tasted like the white wine he'd brought up and her hair smelled as intoxicating as she tasted.

Kye slid his hand under the back of her loose blouse. Her skin was still heated from the bathwater and was silky smooth. With a firm press of his hand on her lower back, she moved to straddle his hips. Eliana couldn't tell who moaned first, but the reverberation moved through both of them. His hands dropped to her hips and she needed no more encouragement to start grinding into him.

The rough texture of his jeans and the firmness of his body between her legs was sending pulses of desire into her. The rocking motion of her hips against his had started applying pressure in just the right spot. Without breaking their kiss, Kye sat up and tucked her more tightly across his lap. His hands dropped lower to grab two handfuls of the lace-covered ass that was making him hard.

Her moans were growing more urgent and when she had to break the kiss in order to catch her breath, Kye used the moment to start nibbling at her throat. He could feel her pulse point pounding beneath his tongue as he tasted her skin. Her breast was soft in his hand and she grabbed a handful of his hair to tip his head back, claiming his mouth again. Eliana's eagerness, if not all-out enthusiasm, when she yanked his shirt off over his head was making his blood surge in a singular direction.

She shifted so her weight was on her knees and when the heat of her V brushed his stomach, a growl erupted through him. Eliana gasped when he gave her backside a hard smack before flipping her over so she was crushed against the mattress. The feel of his muscular torso under her daring fingers was making the fabric of her panties wet with yearning.

"Christ," Kye groaned when her hand moved from his abdomen to his groin where she took hold of his length, the heel of her hand rubbing enough to make his mind go blank.

"I want you," she crooned into his ear, "I want you right now."

"Eli…"

"Don't!" she interrupted and pushed his shoulder enough so they could meet each other's eyes. "I'm already stuck in one game, don't put me in another one. We can't keep pushing ourselves to the edge and not taking the leap. I'm ready Kye, I want you."

"I know you feel ready," he said trying to collect his thoughts. She hadn't yet removed her hand from his erection making coherency hard to come by.

"So, stop fighting it," she whispered against his lips,

her hand rubbing him more intentionally. He let her continue a moment longer, enjoying the sensation before he took her wrist and pinned it above her head.

Using his other hand, he dragged her shirt up. Thinking he was going to pull it off entirely, she raised her arms overhead, but Kye bunched the cloth and let it sit over her eyes, blinding her to the room. He kissed her deeply before his lips moved to her chin, her throat and then her breasts.

There were few sensations she craved more than the feeling of when he took a nipple between his teeth, but when combined with the hand that slid down the front of her panties, she all but lost her mind. Eliana had to grip the post of the headboard to keep herself steady when his thick fingers slid between her folds and began massaging her tender places.

Kye was patient and experienced so he knew the exact moment he found her pearl because every muscle from her neck down tightened and her moan could have lit up Manhattan. He kept his thumb against her jewel and pushed his index and middle fingers slowly inside her. His cock grew painfully hard when he felt how tight she was and when he pushed a little farther, he felt himself freeze. The moment he touched her barrier she let out an involuntary whimper. One that was definitely not in pleasure, but in discomfort.

Removing his fingers, he pulled the shirt from over her eyes, the flush of her cheeks from both arousal and embarrassment. "You're...?" he started to ask and she frowned.

"A virgin? Yeah... You don't need to remind me."

"How is that possible?" Kye asked still laying over her. She was writhing beneath him, either in awkwardness or because she was still thrumming, he didn't know.

"Do you want the scientific answer? I've never had a penis inside me," she said sarcastically.

"Eli," he frowned. "There's never been a guy that you... I mean you never? At all?"

"Despite what we're doing right now, there's not really a 'partial' way to have sex. You don't need to write a song about it or anything... I never found anyone I wanted." Eliana stated, letting out a huff. "That is..." she continued trying to muster her courage, "...not until now. So... just don't stop," she entreated. Her brown eyes were round and reflected both the desire and demand she had for him.

Kye could list a million reasons he should climb off her, run from the house and fling himself into oncoming traffic to prevent another moment of corrupting her. If he was a stronger man he would have. He wasn't a stronger man.

She was moving against him, her body begging for more of the delicious pain his intrusive fingers had given her. He held her face as he kissed her and dug his pelvis into her curve giving her a fresh wave of pleasure. Kye steadied himself before he resumed his attention to her body.

He began kissing his way down her chest, his fingers hooking under the elastic before dragging her underwear down past her thighs and pulling them completely off. His mouth was back to her stomach where her ribs ended and he traveled downward, pausing to dip his tongue into her belly button, her heat dragging along his chest where his fingers were exploring again. Sensing what he was doing when his mouth landed on her pant line, Eliana sat up on her elbows and managed to call out his name before his mouth was on her.

"Kye!"

Immediately the warmth of his tongue on her clitoris made her fall back, one hand gripping at her own hair while the other took hold of his. Kye took her left leg and draped it over his shoulder, pulling her into a more receptive angle, her body now laying wide open to his hungry mouth. The first time he'd smelled her honey aroma he knew she'd taste of it too and she certainly didn't disappoint.

"Oh God," Eliana cried feeling lighting under her skin. Her abdominal muscles were constricting and breathing felt impossible. Eyes squeezed shut, she tried to force every thought out of her mind so she could enjoy the feel of his smooth tongue that was alternating short flicks and long licks.

Kye was clearly enjoying himself as he experimented with his ministrations. He had to hold her hips still after she had bucked so hard he almost lost his position when his teeth nipped at her bud.

She was getting close. Her moans were deeper and she couldn't hold still to save her life. Kye dug his fingers into the tender spots just inside either hipbone and with a few more flicks of his tongue after sucking her into his mouth, Eliana rasped out a long trembling moan that came out in short pants. Her body tensed and released and she all but pushed him away as her pleasure turned to sensitivity.

Her orgasm hadn't fully subsided yet when he flipped her over onto her stomach and drew her hips back so she was bent over in front of him. Her face was buried in her pillow but he could still hear her long groan when his thumb entered her. Still thrumming, her muscles tightened around him and he began rubbing his fingers over her core.

Eliana's second surge came faster and harder than the first and she felt something so deep inside her she didn't know it was there, completely explode with plea-sure. There wasn't an ounce of dissatisfaction left in her when she collapsed on her stomach and Kye withdrew his hand.

He placed a series of small kisses along her spine that gave her chills and he pulled the hair off her neck to kiss those perfect freckles. She made a humming noise of contentment as she turned so her back was against his chest.

"Wow," she breathed and she could tell Kye was smiling even as he kissed the back of her neck. Reaching her arm behind her, she took him by the back of the head and pulled him down to claim his mouth that was still warm from the heat she'd given him.

His hand slid up her bare chest to cup her face, his eyes studying her, looking for any sign that she was unhappy. Her eyes were closed and there was a blissful half-smile on her face. She tried to stifle a yawn unsuccessfully and he reached down to pull the covers over her.

"Wait," she said, her eyes popping open. "What about you…"

"I need to make a phone call," he interrupted knowing where she was going with that sentence.

"A phone call? Right now? You're joking," she said rolling over onto her back. Kye was already standing and retrieved his shirt from the floor before pulling it on. "Kye?" she asked with furrowed brows, the blanket pulled up to her chest. He walked back over to her and tucked a finger under her chin and kissed her.

"Eat that," he said nodding to the plate of unfinished spaghetti. "I've already eaten my dinner." With a wolfish smile and wink, he breezed from the room closing the door behind him. Eliana sat in the dark room for a long moment trying to wrap her mind around his sudden departure.

Ultimately, she scooted herself farther under the covers, tucked a pillow against her chest and fell into a pertinently relaxed slumber.

* * *

KYE HAD SPENT SO LONG STANDING under the icy shower, he was almost positive there would be a water shortage in Maine. Towel drying his hair after his third shower since the night before, he dressed in black jeans and a v-neck shirt. Having taken up residence in Henry's old room that had been completely gutted and cleaned, he grabbed a pair of riding boots from the closet where his clothes hung and quietly made his way downstairs.

It was still early and he saw Eliana's door was closed when he passed. Thinking she was still asleep, he kept moving until he was at the bottom of the stairs. He balked, however, when he saw that Eliana was not only awake, she was dressed and hovering over the table where she was furiously writing on a legal pad.

He cleared his throat as he stood in the archway and she looked up, "good morning," he greeted. Eliana's face was expressionless and she went back to what she was doing. "You're up early," he observed as he walked behind the island of the kitchen.

"Couldn't sleep," she said shortly and opened an empty folder which she started filling with stacks from the table.

"These the new files?"

"Yes."

"The guys must have dropped them off in the night," Kye said picking up a paper and looking it over. "I'll make some coffee," he offered but when he reached the pot he saw it was already full. He started to pour some into two mugs when he noticed it was off.

"It's old," Eliana stated without looking up.

"I'll make a fresh pot."

"Figured you'd like it cold," she muttered. "Cold like your heart."

"What?" Kye asked confused. "What did you say?"

"Nothing."

Setting the pot down he walked over to her and put a hand on her back. She slid away from him to the other side of the table. Kye observed her for a moment. She was refusing to meet his eyes and her posture was rigid.

Hardly the picture of the purring kitten he'd left in bed the night before. "Are you mad?"

"Why would I be mad?"

"You only ask that when you're mad at me. What did I do?"

"Nothing," she said brusquely. "Here," Eliana said handing over the now filled folder she had been compiling. "Two of these men can be released immediately. According to the arrest record they've been held for over twenty-four hours without being officially charged. And this one," she continued as she picked up a thinner file, "he wasn't Mirandized and made aware of his rights. Get the public defender to insist on his release."

"You're changing the subject," Kye noted as he accepted the files.

"This man can plead to the lesser charge of parole violation and serve community service," she rambled on filling his hands with the folders she'd clearly been working on for hours, "and these two men are being held on bond. Have the county surrender them to the bondsman instead of serving time. You'll have to pay legal fees, but they'll be out before the end of the day. I wrote the instructions down." She paused as she looked over the table, "I've got six more I haven't started, but I can have them finished today... maybe tomorrow..."

Kye's hands were loaded with the manila folders

which he promptly set on the kitchen counter and walked over to Eliana. He grabbed for her hand and again she moved away. "Will you stop?" he pleaded and caught her in his arms.

"Don't," she said quietly and turned her head, blatantly refusing to look at him.

"Tell me why you're mad. Is it the cases? I'll take these to Max right away. He'll be thrilled you got this much done already."

"I don't give two shits about Max," she said finally looking up at him. "I'm mad at you!"

"What did I do?" Kye asked defensively. Eliana pulled out of his arms and walked past him. "Is this about last night?" Her silence was his only answer. "Did… did I do something wrong? Did I hurt you?" She turned to stare at him slightly slack-jawed. "If I did something you didn't like, Eli I'm so sorry I just thought…"

"You thought? You mean you actually put brain cells behind what you did?" she asked rudely.

"Excuse me for being a dumbass, you seemed like you were enjoying it," he said feeling entirely confused. Hadn't she been the one begging him? Straddling him? She certainly had seemed like a willing participant…

"Kye," she said pinching the bridge of her nose and squeezing her eyes shut. "I'm not talking about that," she said and Kye felt relief wash over him. "You just… you left. You left the room as if nothing happened and I didn't like that. It made me feel, I don't know… cheap or something."

"Cheap?" he asked once again feeling confusion overtake him. "You're not cheap, Eli."

"I know I'm not, that's why I don't like that you treated me that way. I'm not just a hookup and leave. I told you that. I told you I'd never been with someone because I'd never found someone I cared about that way. I trusted you with that and then… you just left."

"I didn't…" he started to say, but seeing her standing there with a pained expression on her face, he knew that none of his excuses were going to change how she felt. "Come here," he beckoned with an outstretched hand. Reluctantly she took it and he wrapped his arms around her waist. "I didn't leave because I was done with you," he started and she looked up at him with round eyes. "I left because I wasn't going to be able to stop a second time. I don't want to rush anything with you and…"

"And?" she said encouraging him to continue.

"You haven't slept with anyone because you didn't care about them that way. And I… well I have. I've been with women I didn't care about. When they'd had their fill they wanted to be left alone. I'm not proud of it, but it's the truth," he said and Eliana tried to swallow her jealousy. "I'm not good at intimacy I guess. I honestly thought it would be best if I let you sleep."

"I wanted you to stay," she said with a small pout in

her voice. He guided her arms so they were around his neck and she couldn't help the small smile. "Don't leave like that again. I'm not any of the other women you've been with. And if we're being honest, I don't want to hear about any of them ever again." It was Kye's turn to smile. "When we're together, I get all of you or none of you."

"Deal," he agreed and kissed her. She returned the affection, rising on her toes to claim more of his mouth. His hands dug into her back and she broke the kiss only to stifle a yawn. "Am I boring you?" he asked teasingly and she shook her head.

"I've been up since three," she explained. "Coffee only goes so far. Especially that nasty brand you have in the cabinets."

"How about this?" he said running a hand up her back and into her hair, "I'll take the files you've completed to Max. I need to speak to him anyway. I'll be back in an hour and bring you a coffee from the café stand you like."

"ExpressO'?" she asked with excitement. "It's still around?"

"Best espresso in town. Dot left it to her son and retired to Florida about three years ago, but it's still good."

"Mm yes please," she said and kissed his chin. He kissed her quickly before pulling his boots on and gathering the papers he'd set aside. She handed him his coat that had been draped over the back of the dining room chair and he smiled at the front doorway.

"I could get used to this," he said holding her face and brushing her cheek with his thumb.

"Get used to what?" she asked leaning into the tender touch.

"Living with you. Coming home to you. Bedding you."

"Bedding?" she asked with a raised eyebrow. "I think two people need to have satisfaction in order for it to be considered 'bedding'." She was teasing but the heat she radiated gave him chills. Pulling her closer, he tucked the folders under one arm to hold her by the hips.

"You're crazy if you think last night wasn't satisfying for me," he murmured against her lips. She raked her nails over the back of his neck.

"I think we can up the ante next time," she stated in an equally low tone. Kye was smirking.

"Next time?" he asked as her hands ran down his chest and around his back under his coat.

"Mmhm," she hummed and kissed him passionately. He parted only out of necessity and smiled at her one more time before pulling his helmet on and backed his bike out of the parking lot.

Eliana waited until his motorcycle was out of sight before she looked down at the keys in her hand. She'd been able to slip them out of Kye's pocket when they were kissing. Saying a mental prayer, she pressed the button on the fob. The SUV still in the driveway chirped to life.

She had her escape.

8

———

Hardly anyone was at the compound this time of day. Nearly eight in the morning, the only people in sight were the round-the-clock security Max insisted on and any of the drunks who hadn't quite made it to a room. Even the mechanic shop was deserted; the adjoining lot looked like a veritable junkyard of stolen cars waiting to be flipped.

Max wasn't in his office when Kye checked; instead, he found him in the back lot where they kept the dogs. The older man was looking thinner but wasn't toting his oxygen tank like he usually was. Kye didn't know whether this was a good sign or not. His question was answered, however, when he saw the white blunt hanging loosely from his lips. The sickly-sweet scent of Mary Jane wafting in the air.

"Good boy," Max muttered as he rubbed the neck of

the German Shepherd. Taking a neon tennis ball from the animal's mouth, Max hurled it across the yard. The dog took off and chased it down. "She must be scared shitless," Max said, sitting in a lawn chair, and waited with his hand out for the dog to return.

"The dog?" Kye asked dryly.

"Wrong bitch," Max retorted, and Kye's fists clenched. "She up all night on those?" Max asked, gesturing to the files under Kye's arm with his two fingers that now cradled the joint.

"Most of it," Kye answered and handed them over. Max didn't so much as open them before he set them on the ground next to the cooler he was pulling beer bottles out of. Kye accepted the one he was offered but didn't drink from it. "I think more than scared, she's determined. She wants to be done with all of this."

"Of course she does," Max said and took the ball a second time from the dog that had returned. "If she was smart, she'd be more scared." Kye noted a slight grimace when Max chucked the ball toward the far end of the field. It likely would have been imperceptible to anyone else, but Kye liked to think he knew the old man a little better than most.

"She'll have the rest of the files done by tomorrow. She's good. I think you'll be pleased," Kye said, sitting on the cement curb next to Max.

"We'll see," Max said vaguely and let out a long

exhale of white smoke. Kye resisted a gag. "You fuck her yet?"

"Excuse me?" Kye asked with narrowed eyes. Max finally looked at him with a blank expression. His cheeks hollowed while he inhaled again.

"Fuck her," he repeated more slowly, "you fuck her yet?"

"No," Kye answered and lit a cigarette for both relief and to mask the scent of Max's drugs.

"That's a shame," Max stated, only half believing his prodigy. "Bein' she was a tight pussy in high school. She's got that school girl act down pat."

"I wouldn't know," Kye said through gritted teeth, but he did his best to keep his composure. "We've never slept together."

"I find that hard to believe. You mean all these years you never dipped your wick?"

"Not in her oil drum."

Max let out a bark of a laugh that turned into a wheeze. "Shit, boy," Max cursed and banged a fist on his chest to try to clear the cough away. "That was damn funny," Max said, still laughing. He set his blunt down to take a swig of beer. The bottle was sweating with condensation when he rested it in the cupholder.

"How are you feeling these days?" Kye asked as they both watched the dog as it raced around the yard trying to keep the tennis ball from a Doberman that had woken to join the game.

"Like the ass end of a shit hole," Max answered and spat on the ground. "Docs said the cancer wouldn't spread fast, but it's taken my left lung. If I can't manage to kill myself with liver failure, it'll be curtains in six months."

"What about chemo? Radiation?"

"What about it?" Max asked, looking at Kye again. "You think I'm going to let them pump me full of more shit hoping the cancer will kill me, only slightly slower? Nah, boy, this'll be the end of me. I've made my peace with it," Max said, leaning back in his chair. Kye had to admit, Max didn't seem the least bit bothered by his deteriorating health as he lounged in the early morning hours with Mary Jane in his left hand, a beer in his right, and the dog's head now resting in his lap.

"I'm sorry to hear that, Max," Kye said and finally took a swig of his beer.

"You know, I'm inclined to believe a small part of you really is sad to see me go," Max said with a hint of jest in his voice.

"I wouldn't lie about that. There's also part of me that's glad your fat ass is about to croak too."

Max laughed again and lifted his beer in salute. "That's my boy. Honest to a fault. You know I never had a son, but if I did, I'd like to think he'd turn out a bit like you. Better looking, but honest like you."

Kye felt his eyes drop. Despite his building hatred for the man, he couldn't deny the paternal attachment.

"You've built quite the empire, Max. You've got a good legacy here. You should be proud," Kye said, surprising himself with his level of sincerity.

"I owe a big part of that to you," Max admitted, and Kye looked up at him. "You'll run this place well when I'm dead. I've taught you a lot, these last ten years or so. You've got the balls for it."

"You're naming me your successor?" Kye asked more for clarification than for reassurance.

"Sure as shit ain't naming Riggs," Max said loudly. "That prick would blow my fortune on pussy and pills before the year closed out. No," Max said and flicked his joint into the dirt, "it'll be you, kid. You've known it for a while, so don't insult me by acting like you didn't."

"I won't," Kye said, putting out his own cigarette. He couldn't tell if it was Max's melancholy or his own mortality that was putting him in a sullen mood, but the old man seemed a lot colder than usual. "There's been a lot of tension since bringing Eliana into the fold. I thought you might have changed your mind."

"She's a liability for you," Max said, standing and grabbing the tennis ball from the ground. "You and I both know that. Don't let that forbidden fruit get you all tangled up. Mess up your priorities. You didn't flinch when I knocked her around; that's good. Keep yourself detached. You've spent too many years busting your balls to throw it all away for a tight pussy."

"I've no intention of throwing anything away," Kye said honestly. He stood and stuffed his hands into his pockets. The two men fell in step as they walked around the building toward the front entrance. A large semi-truck was pulling in, and the driver waved to Max as he drove past.

"I've got to clear this shipment. Get back to the safe house and make sure she finishes those cases before tomorrow. I'll want to see her when she's done," Max instructed and the truck, surprisingly, pulled up behind the bar instead of toward the warehouse.

"Sure, Max," Kye said watching the truck pull to stop. The driver hopped out and moved toward the back where four security guards were waiting with automatic guns. The door to the back opened and several women jumped down before being ushered inside. Only after did the armed men begin unloading boxes.

"Do yourself a favor," Max said placing his hands on Kye's shoulders pulling his attention back to him. "Fuck her while you still can."

"What do you mean by that?" Kye asked glowering slightly.

"Miss Granville won't be with us much longer," Max said casually, "she's clearing her debt, isn't she?"

"Right," Kye agreed, but he couldn't help feeling there was a double meaning in Max's words.

"So fuck her and get it out of your system. When it's all over, you'll be glad to have that loose end tied up. Now get out of here," Max ordered. They'd walked back to Kye's bike, and he could no longer see the truck behind the building and put it out of his mind. Max was already walking off when Kye started up his motorcycle and headed back.

Eliana had crammed enough of her belongings into her bag to feel satisfied she'd cleared any evidence she had ever been there. She dropped her bag by the door and grabbed the magnetic notepad from the front of the refrigerator.

I'm sorry.

It was all she could think to write as she left it on the counter. Checking her pockets, she remembered her cell phone upstairs. Quickly racing to her old bedroom, she grabbed it from the nightstand. She paused a moment when she saw her old diary still laying on the floor where she'd tossed it the night before. Collecting it, she read the last line of the entry it was open to:

I know without a doubt, I love Kye and I'll never be able to get him out of my system. I'd do anything for him. I love him.

Eliana sank onto the edge of the bed and sighed. Her stomach churned painfully as she imagined Kye's face when he returned, and she was gone. What would happen to him when he reported back to Max that he'd not only left her at the safe house alone, but that she'd escaped? So far, she'd been able to push the thought out her mind, but now it came rushing back like a downpour.

Would the price of her escape cost him his life? Sighing again, she set her diary down. The feeling surging in her felt too much like the night she and her father had fled. They'd left Kye behind amid a spray of gunfire. Wasn't she doing the same thing now? Sentencing him to a firing range?

Closing her eyes, she gripped two handfuls of the bedding underneath her. His scent was still thick in the room from the night before. Her body grew warm at the memory. Her knees squeezed together as her body recalled the feel of his tongue. He'd always been so damn good with that tongue.

It had nearly broken her heart the way he'd admitted he'd been with women he didn't care about. The way he'd said it alluded to more than just casual sex. He'd spent more years as a pawn in Max's game than anyone.

What had that cost him already? It was beginning to become clear to her that when Kye pulled away it wasn't because he was apathetic, it was because he didn't know any other way to be. He'd had to play the soldier for over a decade. He was disassociated, just like anyone else would be.

Yet Eliana knew there was still warmth in him. There was still love. He hid it well, even from her sometimes. When she took a moment to put aside her own fear and anger at her situation, she could understand him a little better. His reserve wasn't cold; it was calculated. The way he withheld from open defiance when Max had hit her wasn't indifference; it was intelligence. Kye was planning his moves, patiently, carefully, strategically.

Maybe she'd spent too much time since they'd been reunited expecting him to be the open, carefree, and passionate boy she'd known in high school. He didn't have the luxury of being open or carefree and his passion wasn't a bonfire; it was an ember. Like magma, it lay dormant inside him. Threatening. Dangerous. Illusive.

Kye had grown up.

She stood a moment later and retrieved her bag from the doorway downstairs and returned it to her bedroom. For better or worse, she'd see this through. Kye needed her. She couldn't leave him to face this alone. Even if that meant the threat of death lingered closer to her than she preferred. Where would she go, anyway? Max had known all along where she was. Or, at least, known how to find her. For all she knew, there was a tracker in the car, and she'd never make the stateline. No, she would stay. With him.

"Kye?" she called when she heard the front door open and close. Bounding down the stairs, instead of seeing Kye it was Grier. He was removing his cut as he looked her over.

"Hi there," Grier said, appraising her. Eliana felt suddenly exposed in her tank top and fitted jeans. "All alone?" he asked, looking around.

"Kye went for coffee," she said, unmoving in the doorway. "He'll be back soon."

"Left you alone? He must trust you," Grier said, walking over to her. Eliana took a step back.

"He trusts you too," she said, hoping to force the implication that he shouldn't do anything to break that trust.

"Yes, he does, we're old friends," Grier replied, his eyes dropping from hers to her chest. "Jez was wrong about you," he muttered.

"In what way?" Eliana asked, realizing she was still backing up when her backside hit the couch in the living room.

"There's a bit of talk about you." Grier looked in her eyes again, his lips pursed. "About what Max will do with you when you're done here. The popular vote is you'll be killed."

"And the unpopular vote?" She swallowed hard.

"There's always room for another Wall Kat. Jez thinks you'll be nothing but trouble, but you won't cause trouble, will you?" Grier ran a hand down her bare arm. She shuddered in unpleasantness.

"I'm not a whore," she said sharply. "I'll not willingly stand on a wall waiting for some horny, drunk biker to decide he wants me." She made to push past him, and he caught her arm.

"You think half of those women stand there willingly?" Grier asked with narrowed eyes. "Willingness isn't a Wall Kat virtue. Obedience is. And if it happens to you, thank whatever god you pray to that I'll find you long before a 'drunk and horny' biker does." Eliana pulled away, her eyes widened at him.

"What do you mean those women aren't willing?" Grier sneered at her question and moved back to the kitchen to grab his cut.

"You're supposed to be the smart one; figure it out," he whispered to her dangerously before slamming the front door behind him.

Eliana sank to the floor, images of the women from the bar flashing in her mind. 'You've no idea what this place really is, do you?' Jez had asked her.

"Oh, God…"

$\mathcal{K}$ye could hear the clattering as he unlocked the front door. He hadn't even remembered locking it when he left. Eliana was in the kitchen scrubbing dishes in the sink. Her back was to him, and he could see her rigid posture.

"Hey," he said, setting the cardboard tray with two coffees on the counter. Eliana stood taller but didn't turn to face him. "What are you doing?"

"Dishes," she said shortly. Oh yeah, she was stressed. He could tell by the terseness in her voice.

"We had a dishwasher installed…"

"Old habit," she interrupted and finally turned to face him. Wiping her hands on a dish towel, she met his eyes. "Did you know?" she asked quietly.

"Know what?" he asked in return. The serious expression on her face had him worried.

"Don't fuck around, Kye, did you know?" she yelled. Kye walked toward her and placed his hands on her shoulders.

"I'm not, tell me what you mean," he said gently. Eliana looked up into his eyes. Her brown ones were searching his blue, trying to find any hint of deception in them. When she found none, she elaborated.

"The women in Jez's bar," she began to Kye's surprise, "human trafficking, Kye." He was quiet for a moment as he processed her statement. "Maybe not all of them, but a lot of them."

"No," Kye said, shaking his head, "we've had Wall Kats for years. It's just part of the club. It attracts that kind of attention."

"Yeah, some, but not all," Eliana said and followed him as he paced around the kitchen island toward the table. "Jez was alluding to it the other day, and then Grier said something…"

"When was Grier here?" Kye asked, rounding on her. She halted in her tracks, and he fixed her with a hard stare.

"About an hour ago," she confessed. "He stopped by, but I'm not sure what he wanted. He was in and out really fast. He said something about the popular vote is that I'll be killed before this is all over, and if not then I'll… I'll…"

"What?"

"He didn't say specifically…"

"What did he say un-specifically?"

"That I'll have a place on the Wall."

"Fuck that!" Kye yelled, and Eliana jumped as his outburst startled her. He crossed to her in two long strides and took her face in his hands. "You have no place on that wall. I'll be dead before I see that happen." She could only nod.

"What about the other women, though?" She tried to swallow her fear. "You can't honestly think all of those women came willingly." Kye stepped away from her and yanked his leather cut off, feeling his body growing hot.

His mind was replaying every scenario he could think of. When the bar had been built in the years before, Max had jokingly called it a harem once. The few times he'd been back at the warehouse during shipments, he'd seen trucks, trailers, semis, making drop-offs, but always in the back. Trucks like the one from earlier… always very late at night or early in the morning.

Kye had never worked bar shipments. That had been territory for the other Demons. Kye's business was always overseas. Riggs specifically handled Jez's.

That prick would blow my fortune on pussy and pills before the year closed out… Max had said. So Riggs would spend his money, not on purchasing prostitutes, but buying women?

Kye let out an angry yell and drove his fist into the wall. Eliana's hand flew to her mouth, and Kye cursed before punching the wall again. The crunching sound of the wall breaking scared her, and she rushed toward him thinking he'd broken his hand. Instead, there was now a fist-sized hole in the wall.

"Stop!" she ordered and grabbed his hand that was red, and his knuckles were bleeding. He yanked his hand away, grabbed the edge of the dining room table, and flung it as though it weighed nothing. Papers and glasses went flying, and Eliana backed away. If Kye's passion was magma, his temper was lava, and he was erupting in anger.

"Fuck! Fuck!" Kye shouted and buried both his hands in his hair. He kicked a chair for good measure before sinking to the floor with his back against the wall. Eliana slowly crossed to the freezer where she removed an icepack and knelt in front of Kye.

"Let me see," she instructed gently, and he held his hand out without protest. Placing the cold pack on his swelling knuckles, she surveyed him. "You really didn't know…"

"Of course not," he snapped, his blue eyes as cold as the compress on his hand. "You really think I'd be okay with human trafficking? Kidnapping women? Raping them?"

"No," Eliana admitted. "No, I know you wouldn't. How could Max have kept it from you all these years?"

"That's how he does things," Kye said, and as his adrenaline faded the pain in his hand found him. "It's how he's kept himself in charge. When we recovered from the Defectors, he split his business into separate entities. The senior riders, the Four Horsemen, were each put in charge of a fragment. I dealt with guns and eventually overseas operations. It kept me busy. I barely know what the others do let alone how they do it. That's the way Max likes it."

"Then who? Who's in charge of bringing women in?"

"It has to be Riggs. The guy you saw at Jez's. He's been managing the Screaming Demon headquarters for a few years now, so Max could be more hands-off. Fuck," Kye cursed again and rapped his head against the wall.

"Stop," Eliana said, placing her hand on his face. "Beating yourself up won't help those women."

"I'm not going to let that happen to you," Kye said, taking her by the back of the neck so she was looking at him. She shrugged.

"How can you stop it, Kye?" she asked, her voice full of emotion. "It's death or prostitution. I don't seem to have a choice in either. Although if I have any say, I think I'll take death."

"You're not going to die, and you're not going to be whored out," Kye said firmly. Eliana stood and took a few steps away from him. "I'll keep you safe."

"You know, you keep saying that," she argued. "No offense, Kye, but you're not doing a very good job so far. I mean, look around. Look at our situation. I'm royally fucked."

"I know it seems like that, but you're not," he said, standing to his feet as well. "I spoke with Max and he confirmed, when he's gone I'm stepping into his role. I inherit the Demons and that means I lay claim to all of the contracts and debts. I'll have the power to dissolve your debt and I'll get to the bottom of what Riggs has been up to. I'll be able to end it all."

"And how long will that take? Max is dying, but how quickly? A month? Six months? Years?"

"He didn't say specifically, but the cancer has spread from his pancreas to his lungs. At the rate he's drinking and smoking, it won't be long," Kye tried to reason. He hated it, but admitting out loud that Max was definitely dying, he felt a twinge of pain. Stifling it for Eliana's sake, he kept his face expressionless.

"I can't bet on that, Kye." Eliana ran a hand through her hair. "I can't have my life hanging on the possibility he'll die before he collects. How long can I stretch this out? Work more cases? I don't think so. You said yourself, Max is tying up loose ends. He knows he's got one foot in the grave, and he's not going to leave any business unfinished. How would that look for his reputation if he left outstanding debts? Am I wrong?"

"No," Kye admitted. Eliana was right. Max was wrapping everything up. He was using Eliana to free as many of his men as he could, but when that was done or they hit a dead end, he'd collect on Eli.

Fuck her while you still can, he had advised. That wasn't a suggestion— it was a threat. Max was going to kill her. Eliana could clearly see the shift in Kye's expression as he came to the same firm resolution she had. Panic surged inside of her, and she felt herself start to sweat.

"I should have left," she said, trembling. "I should have gotten in the car and just left while I could." Now she was the one who was pacing.

"What are you talking about?" Kye asked as he watched her. She dug in her back pocket and held up a set of car keys. Patting his own pockets, he hadn't realized she'd swiped them. His eyes narrowed.

"Eli, give those back," he said, holding his hand out.

"No," she protested flatly. Kye stepped toward her, and she stepped away.

"Don't make me take them away from you," he threatened, his previous coldness returning.

"You can try," she replied. "I'm not messing around

this time, Kye. I'm fighting for my life, and you'll find I don't go as easily as before."

"First of all, you didn't make it easy the last time," he scowled, and she felt a small sense of pride. "Secondly, you're not fighting me for your life. I'll keep you safe."

"I don't believe you," Eliana snapped. "You can say that until you're blue in the face, but you haven't given me one shred of evidence that you will. So far, you're the one who's kidnapped me, locked me in the house, kept me here, watched as Max beat me then manipulated me into staying."

"I manipulated you?" he asked incredulously.

"Yes!" she yelled. "You seduced me, preyed on our history together, and used it as leverage to make me feel sorry for you. I should have left when you were gone and let you face the consequences. I didn't because I… because I…"

"What? Because you what?" Kye asked in equal volume. She'd backed herself into the corner of the room, her feet standing on papers from the overturned table. She was still shaking her head when he stood in front of her. "Because you what?" Kye asked, more gently this time.

"Because I was worried about you. Because I care about you. I didn't want you to get punished for my disappearing… escaping." His hands were on her cheeks, and he kissed her. Eliana neither protested nor reciprocated the kiss as his thumbs brushed her cheeks.

"You still care about me?" he asked with a small grin. She didn't answer. "That's good…"

"Is it?"

"Because I'm still in love with you."

"What?"

"I never stopped loving you, Eliana," Kye said, looking down at her. "I've watched over you since you left. Followed your success in school. Watched you graduate with honors. Read about the first case you took to trial and won. I've loved you every day since we met."

"Kye… I…"

"Trust me now; I won't let anything happen to you. I know Max's game. I can navigate this. For now, we have to act like we're playing along. Let him be distracted with compliance. I've got friends outside his circle. I can make a few calls, get you out of the country where he can't find you. Do you have your passport with you?"

"It's in my bag upstairs," she answered, and Kye nodded.

"That's good," he said, running his fingers through her hair in a soothing manner. "Once my plan is in place, I'll let you in on everything. I promise. No lies. No manipulation. I just need you to trust me a little longer. Can you do that?"

Eliana didn't answer but instead held his gaze for a long moment. He was pressing into her, and she had to admit, the way he shielded her from the room with his size gave her a sense of security. Every nerve in her body was on alert, surging with adrenaline as her fight or flight instinct was ready to trigger at the slightest provocation. Yet here was Kye. Her rock. Firm and sturdy and unrelenting.

She lifted her hand that held the keys, and she handed them to him. Kye took them and slid them into his pocket. "Thank you," he said and took a small step backward. Nodding slightly, she knelt to begin gathering the papers from the floor. "Let me help," he offered.

"I can't say it didn't feel good to see you lose your temper a little," Eliana admitted as they worked to clean up the mess. "I was starting to think nothing got to you."

"There are a lot of things that get to me," Kye confessed as he up-righted the table. "I guess I've gotten used to keeping my feelings in check."

"No pun intended," Eliana said as she helped him to situate the table, "but my how the tables have turned." He grinned. "Remember when I used to be the one who barely showed emotion?"

"I used to think you were impenetrable," he said and pushed the chairs back in before gathering the candlesticks. "We both have learned to handle things in our own way. How to survive. You with your dad and me with Max."

"I can understand," she said, pausing to place her hands on her hips. "I can't be mad at you for it, but I miss the old you. You used to have so much joy in your eyes. Now…"

"Now?" he asked, leaning on the edge of the table. He held his arm out to her, and she tucked herself against him, his hands dropping to her hips.

"Sometimes when I look in your eyes, it's like… you're not there. You're here, but your mind is worlds away. It seems cold, but I know that it's for show. You seem cold because you're distancing yourself."

"Bad habit I suppose," Kye said, feeling he'd adopted the routine subconsciously over the years. Eliana wrapped her arms around his neck.

"If I'm going to trust you," she began as she laced her fingers together, "I need you to let me in. Show me that you have something to lose in all of this too. Don't hide from me."

"Eli," he said, gripping her a little tighter. "I have everything to lose. If something happened to you I… I don't know what I would do."

"That's not good enough," she said firmly. "I need you to know what you would do. If something happens to me, if you think for a moment it's going to come to that,

I need you to kill him. I need you to kill Max. It's either him or me. Promise me that."

Kye swallowed hard. He'd known in the back of his mind it would come to this, but he'd pushed the thought away for as long as he could. "I promise," he said with every ounce of honesty and sincerity in him. "I'll kill Max before I let anything happen to you."

10

Eliana didn't wait for Kye to make the first move. She pressed herself against him, her hips tucked between his parted legs, and kissed him. The whisper of his promise still lingered between them as she pulled his lower lip between her teeth and sucked on it. He let out a hot breath through his nose and cupped a hand on the back of her head.

He hadn't shaved recently, so his stubble scraped at her cheeks in a delicious way. Usually, at a disadvantage, Eliana enjoyed having an upper hand on him as he leaned against the table. Her hands were rubbing the back of his neck, down his chest, and to his waist where she fisted his shirt in her hands.

Kye's hands rubbed up her back and to her sides where his thumbs brushed the sides of her breasts.

Knowing how sensitive she was there, he palmed the tender skin eliciting a moan. Her tongue shot into his mouth, and she grew more aggressive. Kye could feel himself getting hard, remembering the sweet way she tasted, and his hand slid between her legs to cup her heat.

With his lip still between her teeth, she pulled on it, and Kye groaned in both pain and pleasure as she used it to pull him away from the table. When he stood upright, she turned him around, pushed him into the chair to her left, and straddled him in one swift move. The pressure of her crotch on his erection made him even harder, and his hands slid up her back and under her shirt until he pulled it off entirely.

From his seated position, he had a face-full of her gorgeous breasts that he nipped with his teeth. Eliana was grinding down on him, the tightness of her jeans giving her enough friction to stimulate her. What brought her even more pleasure was the feel of him beneath her. It made her feel powerful and sexy to have this level of control. Grabbing a handful of his hair at the roots, she yanked his head backward and started biting at his throat.

"Eli," he hissed when she bit into him. She was grinding harder and faster, and the movement was driving him insane. If she kept this up, he'd have to change his pants. She was biting his earlobe hard enough to distract him from the hand that was moving between them, but the moment she cupped him and squeezed he was entirely aware of her clever fingers. She'd drawn his belt free from the buckle and was unbuttoning his jeans. With the zipper down, her hand slid inside his pants. "Eli!" He took her by the shoulders and pushed her back. She had to stop.

Her eyes looked down and searched his for a moment. Her lips were swollen, and tiny red dots from the scratch of his beard were forming on her chin. Flushed cheeks and dilated pupils, messy hair— she was the picture of erotic. She oozed sex. Resisting the urge to throw her on the table and fuck her right then, he gave her shoulders another gentle push urging her to move off of him.

Eliana bit her lip as she slid off his lap. He sighed and tried to catch his breath. His relief was premature, however, as instead of moving to her feet, Eliana dropped to her knees. Hands on his inner thighs, she pushed his legs open and dug her hand inside his pants.

His erection popped out of his pants like the final note of a jack-in-the-box had been struck and the weasel was free. Any protest he was about to speak was lost the moment her hand wrapped fully around him. His groan was long and startled him at how loud it was.

Apparently, the days of ungratified erections had finally taken their toll.

He looked down at her as she stroked him. Her eyes were glazed, and she was biting her lip to repress her own moan. Clearly enjoying what she was doing, he relented to sit back and let her have her way. God, it felt good. She slid closer to him, pulled his pants and boxers down farther to fully release him, then her mouth was on him.

"Oh… God," he croaked out, head rolling back, hips bucking, teeth gritting, hand burying in her hair. Her mouth was hot and wet, and her tongue lapped at him in eager curiosity. "Slowly… slowly," he managed to say as he held her by the hair. Eliana followed his instructions, slowing the movement as she bobbed her head up and down on his shaft.

His cock was thick, and it pulsed in her mouth. She resisted a gag as it hit the back of her throat, but the more she relaxed her jaw, the easier it was to take his full length. He was patient, and the way he guided her with his hand showed her exactly what he wanted. What he needed. Kye tasted salty, and every groan he emitted moved through him and into her.

She could feel herself creaming, she was so turned on by him. Was this how he had felt the night before? Exquisitely aroused by the effect he'd had? Blissful to be so stimulated by the pleasure his mouth had given her?

Because that was how she felt. When she gently held him with her teeth and her tongue flicked the underside of his tip, he shuddered, abdominal muscles contracting, and she tasted his precum.

So she did it again. Kye gasped and cried her name. Using one hand to grip his base, the other to massage his testicles, her tongue was relentless as it continued to apply pressure to his most sensitive spot. As his orgasm neared, she was finding herself more turned-on and she moaned, the vibration of her humming sending shockwaves through him.

Kye watched her moving against him. The woman between his legs the embodiment of perfection. When she leaned back enough to look up at him, the moment their eyes met, he came completely undone. His orgasm ripped through him, and every muscle in his body contracted as though he'd been electrocuted. She sucked on him until he expelled everything he'd stored up. Even after he was empty, she peppered him with kisses, took his testicles in her mouth, one at a time, and left him panting and completely spent.

Kye was still melted against the back of the chair like a snowman in spring when she turned from the sink where she'd rinsed her mouth. Wiping her lips with the same dishtowel, she felt an overwhelming sense of gratification as she watched him. He tucked himself into his pants but stopped when she moved to straddle him again.

Her self-satisfied smirk was bordering on wicked as she began buckling his belt for him. Thinking it all comes in turns, he began kissing at her throat and reached for her. "Uh-uh," she said, pushing his hand away and zipping his fly. "Let me just enjoy you," she whispered and brushed his lips with hers.

Kye pulled her in for a deeper kiss. "I'm not going to complain," he commented and rubbed her bare back. Her skin was warm and in his relaxed state, he felt himself melting into her. He could feel her still buzzing with arousal. The way she moved against him still. She'd gained a confidence in the way she touched him that made him feel invincible.

Eliana was using him to explore a side of herself that she hadn't allowed herself to before. Knowing this, he felt his own reserve, the small part of him that had always remained detached when he'd been with a woman, break down. The way she cradled his head while she kissed him, slower and softer, touched him. He held her face with one hand and locked eyes with her.

So this was intimacy. Without consciously admitting it, Kye, for the first time, felt safe. And that scared him shitless.

* * *

KYE QUIETLY PEEKED his head around the corner of the living room. Eliana was sprawled on the couch, feet propped on the coffee table next to a mug of tea that was still steaming. Her eyes were fixed on the case file on her lap, and the cap of a red pen was hanging loosely from her lips.

After their tete-a-tete, he'd excused himself to take a shower. He'd lingered longer than was likely realistic, but he'd needed the space to clear his head. There wasn't a moment of his time with her he'd have taken back, but he'd been surprised by the onslaught of emotion that had come with his orgasm.

Images of the women he'd slept with before had flooded him when he'd stood under the hot water. While he had never previously felt any level of guilt, and still didn't, he couldn't deny regret. Like a novice with a gun, he'd trained himself how to be after the recoil. When he'd taken what he wanted, or more often than not, they had taken what they wanted from him, that was it.

Save for a random Wall Kat looking for prestige, he'd never found any woman who wanted to attach themselves to him any more than he desired more than a few nights with them. That wasn't how things worked. The Demons changed arm candy more often than they rotated their tires. He couldn't remember waking up next to a woman let alone wanting to spend a full night with them.

Then there was Eliana. When he'd held her after she'd gone down on him, he felt more connected to her than he'd felt to anyone before. She'd held him, cradled him, and he'd clung to her too. Even after showering, her scent invaded him. He felt her on a cellular level. Like a premonition, he'd imagined waking up in bed with her. Traveling with her. Riding up and down the coast on his bike. Settling down, marrying her. Christ, even having kids with her.

In one moment, she'd ruined him.

Seeing her lounging in the living room, it was like his heart had taken a vacation from his chest and had taken up residence on the couch. He'd never denied he was still in love with her. That love, though, unrequited the last decade, had only grown. Now it sat in front of him in the most vulnerable position it had ever been. Her very life was threatened and likewise, if she died, so would he. Eliana was his one purpose now. He'd never be able to imagine a future without her. He didn't want one.

Taking the opportunity while she was distracted, he pulled the phone out of his pocket and fired off a quick text message to an unmarked number, one he was very familiar with. Given the state of things, Kye didn't have much time to make plans.

And boy, did they need plans.

He'd been completely truthful when he told Eliana that he'd kill Max before he let anything happen to her. In a way, it might be a mercy killing. Max was dying and not in a pleasant manner. Kye had done enough research on pancreatic cancer to know what was in store.

With less than a ten percent survival rate, and that was with treatment, Max was in the last months of survival. When they'd met that morning, Kye had noted the yellowing of his sclera. Jaundice was a sign it had reached his liver as well as his lungs. Even without this, the last push of Max to try to free as many Demons from lockup was his own farewell to the club he'd built from the ground up.

Good or evil regardless, Max was a titan, and there was a melancholy that had crept over the Demons. His condition was widely known, though, maybe not the extent, and with equal parts restlessness and anticipation, change was coming. They all felt it. This level of tumultuous vying for authority hadn't occurred since the Defectors tried to seize control.

Sitting on the back deck, cell phone in one hand, cigarette in the other, Kye contemplated their next moves. Whatever was happening, it would be soon. When Max made the call to end his dealing with Eliana, they'd need to move quickly. Running scenarios in his mind, he knew Max would keep it close to the belt.

Eliana wasn't some nobody living in Pine Hill they could make go away. She was a prominent member of a law firm that was likely already missing her. She could only extend her bereavement leave and vacation time so far before the phone calls would roll in. As soon as people started asking questions, missing her, looking for her, that was when Max would pull the trigger. Either figuratively or literally.

Kye would need to be careful. Methodical. While he had fail-safes in place for himself should he need to flee the country, he didn't have any credentials that would allow Eliana to walk onto an airplane and disappear under an assumed name. Without sufficient time to print up the documents he needed for her, he'd have to think of something else.

That was where the text message came in. Kye could count on one hand the number of people in the world he actually trusted, and as things within the club shifted, the mantle of power hanging in limbo, that list was getting shorter and shorter. Kye needed help.

While Plan A was waiting for Max to kick the bucket, he couldn't keep things in limbo. For all he knew, Max had left explicit instructions with Dhal or one of the goons that should Eliana or any other unfulfilled task be left undone, should he die too soon, for them to finish the task. It was what Kye would have done.

The club was everything to Max. He could be dead ten years, and his bidding would still be done. There were those, like Dhal, who held a particular loyalty not only to the man but to the agenda. It was their kingdom. Their purpose. Their excuse for vengeance, cruelty, and blood. They'd find any reason to inflict pain and punishment wherever they could. Especially if it meant discrediting whoever took over.

While it was a promising prospect to inherit the entire club, it would be several months if not years of unrest before Kye could reasonably take the throne without defiance, disestablishment and likely murder attempts. Riggs could be an issue. Grier too, although the thought made him feel sick.

It only took him a few minutes and two more cigarettes to check on a few things, formulate the rough beginning of an exit strategy when his phone chimed. The anonymous number of a burner phone read a brief message:

The fuck you texting this early for? Kye grinned; he could hear the man's tone in the brief reply.

Do you remember what I said to you in Wexford?
Yes.
Greenlight, mate. It's a go.
For fuck's sake. You can't be serious.

I wouldn't joke about this. Kye sent the text and waited a long moment. He pulled out a fourth cigarette and struggled to light it. He abandoned the task when his phone finally buzzed with the response he was waiting for.

Well, it's been a good run. Jeronimo!

11

According to modern science, there were seven distinct forms of mental disorders and behavioral health diagnoses. The most common among them being anxiety, mood, and psychotic. As Eliana stood staring out the window in the kitchen, arms crossed, bare feet pressed firmly into the tile, she wondered what she was afflicted with more: anxiety, mood, or psychosis.

It had been two days since she'd sent back the last of the cases Max had provided. She'd fallen into a steady routine for nearly a week. Boxes would come in, and she'd send them back out. Working the defense had kept her mind occupied. She'd been able to distance herself from the crimes, most of which were petty theft, armed robbery, possession. Two, in particular, had afflicted her. Murder. It had taken three straight nights and endless amounts of coffee, but she'd managed to sabotage the prosecutor's case. They would walk. Two days ago, the boxes stopped coming, and she hadn't heard a word from Max.

Yanking the fridge open, she stared vacantly at the contents. Kye, the dutiful prison warden, had kept it stocked with anything she could have wanted. Fresh vegetables and fruits, bottles of sparkling water, organic gluten-free pasta... Eliana sighed as she grabbed a beer and the bakery-fresh cheesecake. Tossing the plastic dome lid aside and popping the top of the beer, she sat at the counter, drank from the bottle and ate from the tray.

Add an eating disorder to her list of current afflictions.

The front door opened and closed, but she didn't bother looking up. She knew it was Kye. His bike had rumbled into the driveway nearly thirty minutes ago, but he'd paced the front yard talking on his cell phone for a long while. She'd watched him. Black boots trekking through the muddy yard, his khaki cargo pants fitting well over his ass where her eyes had lingered, tight-fitting white shirt under his black leather cut that was adorned with patches and brands from the Demons. He'd worn his hair down that day, the long strands well past his shoulders now. In the gray afternoon, he looked ethereal against the din.

"That kind of day?" he asked, setting his cut on the counter next to her. She made a humming noise of agreement, and he kissed her on the top of the head before fetching a beer for himself. "You going to save me any of that?" he asked, gesturing to the cheesecake with his bottle. Eliana's reply was a large bite where she licked the fork clean. "Then again I could watch you do that all day…"

"What happens when I run out of cheesecake?" she asked, raising an eyebrow. "Got anything else I can put in my mouth?" Kye choked on his beer, spittle running down his chin and staining his shirt. Eliana smiled triumphantly. Their game of sexual tug-of-war was likely the only thing keeping her from snapping. The boredom and lunacy of waiting were only adding to the tension and anxiety that had built up in her. So why not add sexual tension to that.

"I can think of something," he said, setting his bottle aside and tossing her a wink. She grinned and watched as Kye pulled his shirt off and began rinsing it in the sink. Eliana couldn't help biting her lip. With his back to her, she could see every curve of muscle as his shoulder blades moved. He'd always had a darker complexion than her, and the hours he'd spent outside gave his skin a more bronze hue. Smooth and chiseled with two dimples on his lower back, she imagined how much better his skin would look covered in fingernail marks.

"Do you have any news?" she asked, trying to pull her thoughts back. "I don't know how much longer I can stand the silence. I need something. Anything." Her voice was sharp and had an edge of pleading. Kye wrung his shirt out and tossed it over his shoulder before turning.

"I'm sorry, I don't," he answered. "Max has gone quiet since yesterday. Last I heard he said he'd send more your way when he has it." The white shirt was still wet, and her eyes followed a droplet of water that ran down his chest, over his pectoral, down the center of his prominent abs and soaked into the elastic band of his underwear that peeked out above his pants.

"It seems like he's stalling," she commented. "Like he's trying to make up his mind about something."

"Could be," Kye said, retrieving his beer. "He wants you nervous. He wants you to be afraid. It's what keeps him in power."

"From one control freak to another, it's working." Having lost her appetite, she dropped her fork with a noisy clatter. "I spent eighteen years of my life feeling trapped in this house, and now look where I am? Trapped again."

"Come here," Kye said, tossing his wet shirt aside and opening his arms. Eliana stood and let him embrace her. His skin was warm, and traces of a heady cologne lingered on his neck. She closed her eyes and breathed him in. "I'm going to get you out of this. Soon."

"I know. I can see you're working on things," she said, looking up at him. She loved the way his chest pressed against hers. Lowering her hands to his hips, she absently fiddled with the loops of his jeans. "Are you going to tell me who you keep talking to on the phone?"

"I can't," he said with an apologetic tone. "I know it makes you feel helpless, but the less you know the better. For now, just try to keep your mind off things." She raised an eyebrow at him. "I know, it's like asking you to hold the ocean back with a broom…"

"It'd be easier to give myself a root canal."

"Want me to get the pliers?"

"Jerk," she teased and gave him a playful shove. Kye took her by the hips and hoisted her onto the counter before digging his fingertips into her side. "No, no!" she shrieked and tried to push him away, but he was merciless as he tickled her. Both pushing him away and pulling him closer, she ended up tackling him to the ground, and he both groaned and laughed as they flopped on the tile floor.

"That's not fair; you have bony elbows," he protested as she straddled him. Her face was flushed, and she was smiling from ear to ear. He sat up, hands holding her back so she didn't fall backward. Her smile faltered as they locked eyes, and their intimate hold on each other became charged. "God, I want you," Kye muttered when his eyes dropped to her lips.

"I want you too," Eliana whispered and kissed him. His grip was fierce, and the air rushed out of her as he crushed his chest against hers. "What is it?" she asked when he pulled away. "What's stopping you?"

"Nothing," he lied and lifted her to her feet before standing. Her eyes were narrowed, and he took her chin between his thumb and index finger. "I'm going to have you," he said, more like a promise than anything else. "I'm going to take you in every way a man can take a woman and probably some new ones." She couldn't help the smile. "Not until it's safe."

"Why?"

"Because I want you so bad it's killing me. Gives me drive to get you the hell out of here."

"So let's go," she pleaded. Kye's eyes dropped. "What? What aren't you telling me?"

"Eli," he began, and she stepped back from him. It was easier to think when he wasn't touching her. "I wasn't just out for a ride this morning. I wanted to scout the roads."

"And?"

"It's not good."

"Just tell me!"

"Max isn't just covering his bases; he's turned the town into a veritable blockade. He owns the county patrol, and they've got squad cars posted on the north and south bridges."

"What about the eastern road? If we leave town, we can drive the coastal highway."

"That seems to be the only clear path, but it's throwing a wrench in my plans. With only one escape route, the minute I get you out of town they'll know exactly what road we took."

"Why all the paranoia? This can't be for me. Max already has me here."

"It's not. With Max assembling his predecessors, all hell is breaking loose. Or rather, breaking in. Come the end of the month, every chapter of the Screaming Demons will have members in town."

"How many?"

"We've got thirty chapters from here to London."

"Fuck," Eliana said, pressing the heels of her hands into her eyes.

"Don't get discouraged; it may end up being the distraction we need," Kye said, placing his hands on her shoulders. "If we time it right."

"If we don't, all Max has to do is show my picture around, and I've got a lynch mob on my back."

"Enough," he said, holding her face, "you let me worry about that. The only thing you'll have on your back is me." That earned him another smile from her, and he kissed her forehead.

"Not if you don't put a shirt on. You'll be the one on your back," she muttered as she turned around and made for the stairs. Kye grinned and gave her rear end a hard smack that elicited a yelp from her.

"We'll take turns," he whispered in her ear before he raced up the stairs in front of her. Eliana nearly drew blood she bit her lip so hard. If the tension of having her life hang in the balance was doing nothing, it was making her hornier than a cat in heat. God how she longed to take out all her frustrations on that man.

* * *

ELIANA WASN'T MAKING this easy on him. Thinking she was asleep, he'd stayed up late into the night keeping watch over the house. It was the only way he could know who may be stopping by. It wasn't uncommon these last few days for one of Max's enforcers to swing by to ensure everything was fine. Although Eliana still wore the tracking bracelet on her ankle, Max wasn't going to take any risks.

So here he sat, on the back deck smoking a cigarette and watching her through the sliding glass door. The way she stood in the laundry room folding clothes from the dryer and putting them into the basket was easily the most erotic thing he'd ever seen. Her hair was pulled into a bun on top of her head, wisps of hair sticking out in every direction. No makeup but her skin glistened as though she'd recently applied lotion.

She was wearing a white tank, like the ones he wore under a dress shirt, and barely-there blue lace panties. Likely under the same assumption that he was sleeping, he'd never seen her prance around the house in so little clothing. He could tell, even from his distance, that she wasn't wearing a bra, and every time she bent to retrieve another article of clothing from the dryer, her supple breasts moved freely under the thin fabric. The darker skin of her rosy areolas came to a peak where her nipples budded.

Kye's hand wandered beneath his belt line while he watched her. Earbuds dangled from her ears, and her hips were moving subtly as she undoubtedly swayed to the music. When she turned to start another load of wash, he got a full view of her ripe ass. God how he wanted her bent over like that while he drove himself into her. Kye groaned as she stood and reached for the top shelf to grab the laundry detergent. Her shirt rode up, and he caught a quick glimpse of the heart tattoo on her hipbone.

Having seen it only in passing while he'd been preoccupied with her more heated parts, he now couldn't get his mind off it. He wanted to suck on that heart until it bruised. Maybe that was the reason he was forcing this delay. She wanted him. He could smell it on her, and she'd done everything but show up in his bed naked and begging for it.

That was a tantalizing thought.

Kye wasn't going to fuck this one up. How much damage had he done already? If he'd done a better job protecting her these last few years, she likely wouldn't be in this situation. The last thing he wanted now was to have her like some quickie one-night stand simply because the stress of their predicament demanded it.

No. He wanted her slow. Languid. And Passionately. He wanted her stretched out on her stomach while he slid into her from behind. He wanted her on her back, spread open and panting while he rocked his hips relentlessly. He wanted her against the wall of the shower, wet, hot, and slippery. Wanted his tongue to taste every inch of her from neck to navel, from throat to ankle, and then all over again.

Grinning, bemused with himself, he joked, I'd have her in a car; I would have her in a bar. I'd have her most anywhere, bent over, on top—I don't care.

Eliana shut the door to the washer and gathered her things before leaving the room. The light switched off, and the glow left Kye in complete darkness on the porch. Closing his eyes, he pumped his hands a few more times before grunting as he ejaculated. His body shook for a moment as his high receded, and he put his cigarette out.

Kye waited until he was sure she wasn't around before he slid inside and pulled his now sullied pants off in the laundry room, lifted the lid to the running washer and tossed them in to rid the evidence from his trousers. He noted that she'd folded a few of his things and left them sitting on the dryer. Among them were a pair of gray sweatpants he pulled on. They were still warm.

Poking his head around the corner, he saw Eliana disappear into her bedroom, closing the door only half-way. Thinking himself game for a little mischief, and still riding the high of his hurried and self-gratified orgasm, he wondered if he'd catch another glimpse of ass cheeks if he snuck to the doorway in time.

Gently pushing it open, he saw her standing with her back to him. That glorious lace-covered bottom still peeking out at him. Her earbuds were discarded on the end table, and she was reading what he knew was her old diary.

Stepping too hard on a floorboard that creaked, Eliana turned with a gasp when she heard and saw him standing there. Her eyes were red and dripping with tears. Kye sobered abruptly.

I'm a jerk in a box; I'm a jerk in my socks. As I jerk here I stand, with nothing else but my dick in my hand…

12

"**B**aby, what is it?" Kye asked, rushing forward and taking her into his arms. She was still clutching the white book in her hand, and she sniffled a few times against his chest before pulling back.

"It's stupid," she said, sniffling again and sitting on the edge of her bed. He hated himself for noting she was now eye level with his crotch, so he sat next to her.

"Tell me," he encouraged and began rubbing her back.

"I needed something to keep me busy, something to occupy my mind." She gestured to the diary. "I thought reading would help." A fresh wave of tears sprang from her eyes, and she buried her face in her hands. He let her cry for a moment, gently stroking her hair. "Do you have any idea how much I loved you?" she asked when she had regained her voice.

Kye swallowed hard. It occurred to him simultaneously that she was both confessing she loved him and using the past tense to do so. Did that mean she didn't love him anymore?

"You came into my life so unexpectedly, and it's like the moment you did, everything else stopped." She wiped her nose with the back of her hand. "I can read it all here. I bought this journal at the start of my junior year. It's all 'Harvard, Harvard, Harvard' and then… just you." She began flipping through the pages as though it was a catalog of events. "Kye and I went to the arcade. Kye stole my favorite pen again. Kye surprised me at work. Kye and I spent the whole night in the treehouse. Kye, Kye, Kye!" Slamming the book shut, she tossed it onto the ground.

"I'm sorry," he said, not knowing what else to say. Although agitated by his touch, she shrugged until he removed his hand. "You're mad at me?"

"Yes," she said, standing again. "No," she contradicted and pinched the bridge of her nose. "Do you remember what I told you about my dad?" She abruptly changed the subject. "That I didn't so much miss him as the idea of him?" He silently nodded. "My dad was never there. He thought he was, but he wasn't. Now that he's dead, I have to face some hard truths. I don't think I ever loved my dad. I loved the idea of having a dad. He's dead, and he'll never be what I hoped he would be one day. That dream is gone and buried with him. The only thing I can do now is grieve the loss of something I never had."

"You deserved better than what your dad gave you…" Kye started, but she waved her hand to dismiss his condolences.

"I'm not talking about my dad," she said in an even tone. Kye fell silent. "Reading through my old diary was like reading about another lifetime. I was a different girl then. I was so full of hope. You were a different boy."

Kye swallowed hard and folded his hands in his lap. He couldn't deny she was telling the truth. Thinking back to that kid who'd first moved to Pine Hill with a duffle bag and a chip on his shoulder. Had he ever truly thought he could rescue both of them from this fate?

"I loved you so much, Kye," Eliana said and pressed a hand to her throat, "but just like my dad, I have to grieve the idea of you now."

"You… you never really loved me?" he asked, surprised that his voice was cracking. Eliana looked startled.

"No, Kye," she said with new tears. "I loved you very, very much. What I mean is… the Kye that I said goodbye to on the side of the road that night… the Kye that I danced with at prom… is not the same Kye who walked back into my life three weeks ago." She took a deep and shaky breath before expelling it. "The Kye I loved is gone. I can't keep trying to recreate him in you. I have to grieve him like someone who has died. Do you understand?"

"Yeah." He cleared his throat. "You're right, I'm not the same person I was. When I was younger, I would have gone in guns blazing to keep you safe. I sure as hell never would have let things get this far." When he wiped a hand over his face, he wasn't shocked to find tears had started falling from his eyes.

"When we were kids, you seemed so… adventurous," she said with a small laugh. "You brought color into my black and white world. Like that scene where Dorothy first arrives in Oz. You were the escape I needed from the hell that was my house… this house." She gestured to the room.

"You were that for me too," he admitted. "I'd been on the move for so long. Changing houses, schools, siblings, parents. Nothing was ever the same for more than six months. I knew that no matter what, my feelings for you were a constant. You were my rock. The one thing I wanted to hold on to."

"We had lives where we could be that for each other," she said. "I was strong and confident in the course my life was taking. Like a ship on the ocean. My compass pointing north. You blew in like the wind."

"Blew you off course?"

"No," she countered. "Urging me forward. It was for that, I fell in love with you. That was ten years ago, though. Now… you're not the wind in my sails, Kye. You're the edge of a cliff. Dangerous. Terrifying. You're the end of the line."

"That doesn't change how I feel about you, though," he said, looking up at her. "Eli, I was, am, and always will be completely in love with you."

"I know," she whispered, still clutching her throat. "I don't… I don't know if I can say that back."

Had he stopped to think about it, he would have known that was true. He'd followed her life this last decade, but she'd moved on, hadn't she? It was his fault. He'd intentionally kept himself hidden from her, and now he had to face the consequences. In the last ten years, he'd become nothing but a stranger with a familiar face to her.

"You know who I've become," he said, regaining some of the strength of his composure. "I've become a criminal, a liar, a kidnapper. I've killed people, sold drugs, smuggled weapons, and now I find I'm involved with a club that traffics women…" He sighed heavily.

"Those are things you've done," Eliana agreed. "I'm not sure that it's an exact description of who you are, though." She wrapped her arms around herself feeling cold as he stared blankly at her. "I see other things in you. You still have kindness. I see it in the way you treat me. Morality. You know right from wrong, trying to find the greater good even if that means bending and breaking rules. I see it all the time in the courtroom. You're hard like you're made out of stone, but there's still gentleness. You still have a heart hidden under all those scales."

Kye held his hand out to her, and she hesitated before taking it. Gently pulling her toward him, he placed her hand on his chest over his heart. "It's there," he assured her. Rising slowly, his hand still laid over hers, he looked down into her eyes. "Is this a man you can love? Not for what I was, not for what we used to be, but as I am now?"

Eliana didn't answer at first. She didn't want to lead him on, so she took her time considering his question. Staring at his hand which lay over hers, the size difference between them amazing her. That was Kye, wasn't it? He trumped her in every way. Outsized her, shielded her, barricaded her from the world. Where once he'd set her free, now he kept her concealed.

"I don't know," she answered finally. She could feel his heart pounding beneath her hand. "I've only just realized I need to let go of who you were. Give me time... time to learn who you are now. Maybe, when your boss isn't considering killing me."

"I won't let that..."

"Let that happen?" she interrupted, looking up at him

with round eyes. "I'm trusting you. My life is in your hands." At the declaration, his love for her trust, he felt the sudden weight of responsibility. Lifting both of her hands to his mouth, he kissed them.

"Your life is in my hands and my life," he started before placing both of her hands over his heart, "is entirely in yours."

KYE WOKE with a start when he felt his phone vibrating in his pocket. It took him a moment to reorient himself. At first, he couldn't remember where he was, and the dark room did nothing to help. It wasn't until he felt the body stirring next to him that he remembered.

He and Eliana had stayed up half the night talking and must have fallen asleep while reclining on the headboard. She was tucked under the covers next to him facing the wall, so he did his best to slide out of bed without disturbing her. It was raining outside, and as she'd left the window slightly ajar, there was a dampness to the air that made him shiver when he stood.

His phone was lit up with a text from the burner phone he'd been texting for the last several days. It was good news. Short on allies, Kye was grateful at least one thing was coming into place. Looking down at Eliana, he pulled the covers a little higher over her shoulder and dropped a kiss to her temple. While he desperately wanted to climb back into bed if only to feel her warmth against him, he knew he had work to do before morning.

When he moved toward the door, his foot caught on something. Cursing under his breath, he managed to stop himself from tripping. Retrieving the intrusive object from the floor, he found it was the diary Eliana had discarded from the night before. He tucked it under his arm as he made his way downstairs. In the living room, he flicked on the single lamp in the corner and set to invade her privacy.

Eliana hadn't been lying. The first third of her diary had been eloquently written rants and babbles about her application process to Harvard. He could track almost to the day when they'd met. Even the color of ink she wrote in changed from black to blue, although he doubted that signified intentionality.

I met a boy today in SAT Prep. I'd seen him a few times, but we hadn't spoken directly. I don't do very well with boys, especially attractive ones. His name is Kye, and he's beautiful. I've never seen eyes as blue as his. All icy and cool with darker rims. Like an iceberg on the Caribbean. The way he told Missy off made my whole year...

Kye found himself smiling at the memory. Part of him was grateful she had been as affected by him when they first met as he was with her. If only she felt that way now. His heart constricted painfully when he remembered her admission that she didn't love him and didn't know if she could.

He read through a few more memories before he stopped himself. Hadn't this been exactly what she was talking about? They could spend their days reminiscing about their past, being angry at the years they were cheated of, or they could accept the way things were now. The way they were now.

Sitting back in the armchair, Kye let himself feel a moment of grief for the childhood they no longer had. He also had to admit to himself maybe he was living for the past too. Was that the source of his reluctance to give anything up? He seemed to be expecting an awful lot from Eliana without much in return. He was expecting her to operate on promises and trust when her life and livelihood hung in the balance.

Although she didn't know he knew, Kye had monitored the emails she'd been sending and saw the letter of resignation she'd sent her law firm that morning. Even Eliana was aware that should they both survive this, there was no going back. While her name wasn't on the records, she had still participated in freeing a long stream of criminals. Maybe it was her conscience, but she wouldn't be able to just forget what she'd done here. Like it or not, her hands were dirty too.

Readying himself to put the book aside, he satisfied one last curiosity and read her final entry. Expecting it to be something near prom, he was shocked to see it was a recent entry.

Hello Old Friend, it began.

Don't hate me for leaving you behind. I was rushed away from home without warning. Had I had the chance to retrieve you, I never would have left you behind. Can we talk? I'm quite possibly the closest I've ever been to death, and yet I feel more alive than ever. Does that make any sense at all? Staring down the barrel end of a gun, I can't shake the electricity that is filling me. My life has been a series of predictables, textbooks, laws, and standards. Yet here I am, on the opposite end of the law I swore to uphold, working for a crime lord and living with a criminal. My every waking moment is full of suspense and danger and, God help me, it's full of passion like I've never known. I quit my job today. For a myriad of reasons, but mostly because I will never be the same after this. Whatever is in the water, I drank from the well, and I'm forever changed. I know things about myself, exciting things, that just make an office job seem so obsolete. I won't abandon my passion for the law and protecting the innocent, but neither will I deny that I am— for better or worse— so much more than I thought I ever could be. I guess I have Kye to thank for that. Sexy, stoic, resolute Kye with the serious brow. He's changed, you know. Not like the happy youth I once loved. No, he's very different. And not entirely for the worse.

Kye closed the book and smiled. Whether she realized it or not, he could tell in her words, she was falling in love with him again. Not the old Kye, not the kid, the man. She'd once called him her hero. He could be that for her again. Not by repetition, but by evolution. He'd grow into the man she needed him to be.

He'd win her back.

---

13

*E*liana opened her eyes when she felt something shift underneath her. With a jolt, she sat up and scrambled off the bed. In the process, her legs tangled in the silky sheet, and she tumbled toward the floor. Attempting to catch herself, she flailed an arm toward the nightstand only to send the contents of the top spilling over as they, and she, crashed to the ground.

"Ow," she groaned, laying prostrate on the carpet. Hearing a chuckle behind her, Eliana rolled over and saw Kye with his head resting on his upraised arm laying on his side facing her.

"I pictured waking up next to you very differently," he noted, and she huffed at him. "You alright?"

"I'll live," she grumbled and kicked herself free of the sheets. The irony of her statement wasn't lost on either of them. Kye reached for her hand and pulled her back into bed. Unresisting, Eliana slid back under the covers next to him, both laying on their sides facing each other.

The weather hadn't improved in the night, and they could both hear the pattering of rain on the roof and windows. The wind must have picked up because there was howling in the distance. Kye, having closed the window the night before, was grateful. Had he not, the carpet likely would have been soaked.

"I'm surprised you stayed," Eliana commented as she absently picked at the sheets, her eyes intently focused on the task.

"I guess I haven't built the reputation of staying," he agreed and rubbed the sleep out of his eyes. "Can I tell you something?" he asked, and she looked up at him with expectant eyes. "I've never slept with a woman before." He chuckled when her brows knit together, and her lips pursed. "Not in that way," he elaborated. "I mean, I've never fallen asleep and stayed the entire night with anyone."

"That doesn't make sense," Eliana said. "Sleeping next to someone doesn't seem nearly as, I don't know, serious as having sex with them."

"To you, maybe," he replied. "It's different for people I guess. For you, maybe having sex is the most personal thing you can do; for me, it's sleeping beside someone. I don't like having my guard down around people. I was this way in foster homes too. Bad shit happened to kids when they were sleeping. What position is more vulnerable than allowing someone to have access to your sleeping body?"

"I can't argue that," Eliana answered. Her bottom lip sank between her teeth, and she trailed a finger along the arm he used to prop his head up. "So why me then? I could have just as easily killed you in your sleep as anyone else."

"You could have," he agreed with a chuckle. "But if it was going to be my last act, falling asleep beside you, I would have died happy."

"Are you trying to be romantic?" she asked with a hint of accusation in her tone. He scooted closer to her.

"Are you feeling romanced?" he asked in return with an equal tone of voice.

"No, but it was a sweet thing to say," she confessed. His eyes searched her face for a few seconds and for the briefest of moments, she saw a long, familiar glint of mischief in his eye that made her breath hitch. It reminded her so much of the boy she used to know.

"Thanks for letting me live," he said, and they both smiled. She seemed to catch herself, though, and as quickly as it appeared, her smile fell. "What are you thinking?" he asked, lifting a hand to tuck a bit of hair behind her ear.

"I quit my job yesterday," she replied with a hard swallow. Kye raised both eyebrows in feigned surprise.

"Let's face it, Kye, on the off-chance Max lets me live, he won't let me off the hook. He'll want me to keep working for him until he dies. If that takes another six months, I can't draw out my vacation that long. I've already received two emails from my boss asking how I'm doing."

"That doesn't sound too bad. Maybe he's just concerned," Kye suggested. To his dismay, Eliana rolled out of bed, much more gracefully this time, and stood. He had to remind himself to be patient when his instinct told him to reach for her and draw her back into bed.

"I've no doubt my colleagues are concerned," she said, digging through her suitcase for fresh clothing. "Time moves quickly in the courtroom. If I'm gone for an unforeseeable amount of time, then that's one less person working a caseload. One less pair of eyes and set of hands. They need all the help they can get. We were short-staffed when my dad got sick, and with me gone they're likely desperate. No..." she said, trailing off as she settled on an outfit. "It's best for them to move on. Find someone else. Someone more reliable and..." She wanted to say, 'someone likely to live' but couldn't force the words out.

"Hey." She jumped, startled again. She'd been so lost in thought she hadn't noticed Kye slink out of bed and cross to her until his arms were wrapping around her waist. She placed a hand over his arm but didn't sink into the embrace. "I'm sorry, Eli. I know that job was important to you."

"It was," she agreed and slid out of his arms as slowly as she could so as not to give offense. "A lot of things used to seem so important. Now, I just want to live to the end of the day. It's hard to feel hope for the future when I know I'm not guaranteed one."

"Please don't talk like that," Kye asked pleadingly. "It makes it sound like you have no faith in me to keep you safe. I told you, I'd kill Max before he can hurt you again."

"You can promise that, Kye, and a thousand other things. That doesn't set it in stone. What if Max hires a contractor to kill me ten years from now? What if the next box of case files has a bomb in it? Or in my car? What if the Chinese take-out I order is poisoned?"

"Easy," Kye began. "I'll have the boys open the boxes outside first before they ever get to you. We won't drive your car, and we'll order pizza, not Chinese. Much harder to poison pizza." His joke earned him another smile. He hesitantly placed his hands on her shoulders and slid them up to her neck to cradle her face. "And in ten years' time, I will still be following you, and I will kill anyone who tries to harm you."

"That's sweet," she sighed, "a little creepy," she teased. "But sweet." Standing on her tiptoes, she kissed him in the gentlest of brushings of her lips to his. He savored it even long after she'd disappeared into the bathroom to shower.

Yeah. She was definitely falling in love with him again.

KYE HAD BEEN WAITING all day for a break in the rain, and when it finally came just before dinner, he had hauled Eliana from the couch in the living room and insisted they go out.

"What about the monitor?" she asked as he dragged her toward the door. Remembering the bulky thing, he phished the key out of his pocket, knelt to unlock it, and slipped it from her ankle before depositing it in the bowl near the door.

"Come on," he said, taking her hand. She was surprised when he walked them straight past the cars to his bike.

"What if it starts raining again?" she asked when he handed over a helmet.

"Afraid to get wet?" She narrowed her eyes. Sliding on to the back of the bike, Kye took his place in front of her, and they were off.

It didn't take long for her annoyance to melt into joy. It felt good to be out of the house. Cooped up for nearly two weeks straight either bent over the dining room table or in the living room, she was starting to go crazy. Perhaps Kye had too, and that was why he insisted they go out to eat.

Although the town had changed dramatically, she could still navigate the streets, and she felt a small shiver of anticipation as they neared one of her old favorite places. The park. Even before she'd met Kye, it had been one of her favorite places. Having been built long before she was born, it was one of the few places in town she had that held memories of her mom.

At the next stop light, she could see it on their right. There was the play equipment that had been repainted but still stood the same. A new swing-set was installed, and the landscape had shifted to include two water fountains and a splash pad. Her eyes searched trying to place her finger on what seemed so different. The moment she realized what it was, she gasped.

"Oh my God," she cried, hand flying to her mouth.

"What is it, Eli?" Kye yelled as she jumped off the back of the bike and ran toward the playground. Ignoring the traffic, he zipped through the red light and flipped a U-turn, drove up and over the curb and parked on the sidewalk. He tossed his helmet recklessly onto the back as he chased her. "Oh," he sighed when he caught what had caused her distress.

"They tore it down," she said in a quivering voice, tears already in her eyes. "Our tree," she said, although she didn't need to elaborate. Where once the ancient and wonderful willow had towered over the far end of the park and dipped half its branches into the lake, now stood a canoe and kayak rental shed and a small window that read "Ivan's Icees". Though it was closed now, Eliana was positive the icees tasted like shit.

"There was an ugly storm that blew through town about five years ago. A lot of trees went down, and a few powerlines were damaged. After that, the mayor put utility crews to work tearing down anything they thought looked like it may be rotting. I'm sorry I didn't tell you; I had kind of forgotten. I should have warned you," Kye apologized and wrapped an arm around her shoulders, and he felt her trembling.

"I shouldn't be this upset over a stupid tree," she berated herself as she wiped her tears away. "I guess I just... wish I could have said goodbye. Is that stupid?" she asked, turning to face him. He held her tightly, tucking her head under his chin.

"It's not stupid at all. You didn't have many things in your life you could count on, Eli. Not many things to rely on. In a small way, you relied on that tree. It was always there when you needed it, wanted it. It held you up and covered you whenever you called on it, never asking questions or judging you. It was a friend in its own way. And now it's gone. That's a loss, and you cry all you want over losing a friend."

"How do you understand me so much better than even I can understand myself?" she questioned as she looked up into his eyes. He gave a half shrug and wiped one of her tears away with his thumb.

"Because I love you," he said softly, "I make it my business to know you." She took a sharp breath, mouth opening to speak, but only a small croaking sound from the back of her throat came out. Her instinct had been to reply, but she'd caught herself. He gave a small smile of understanding and took her hand. "Come on, let's walk over."

"I don't know if that will help any," she said, but she didn't resist as he led the way past Ivan's shitty Icees and down toward the water. The landscapers were still clearly renovating parts of the park because there were several trucks parked in the adjoining lot. Some were filled with gravel and large boulders while others had mulch, shrubbery, and trays of spring perennials waiting to be planted.

"Here it is," Kye said when his feet hit a large patch of dirt that was muddy and soft from the rain. "This must have been where the trunk was. You can feel the ground give way." He gave a couple of bounces on his heels to prove a point.

"Fresh plot of earth," Eliana said, wrapping her arms around herself. "Promise me that if I die, you'll bury me here."

"What?" Kye asked, turning abruptly to look at her.

"Ground is soft," she said, kicking at it with the toe of her shoe. "Wouldn't be hard to dig a grave…"

"I swear to God, Eliana, if I ever hear you talk like that again I'll… I'll…"

"Kill me?" she asked ironically as she looked up at him. Kye's eyes were ablaze with anger, and his nostrils were flaring with the strain of his rapid breathing. Hands balled into fists, he marched toward her. When she didn't recoil in the slightest, his temper surged.

"I'm not going to kill you," he spat, staring down at her. "But so help me, I'll spank the defeatist tone right out of you." She still stared blankly at him. An idea seemed to strike him so he turned on his heel and ran toward the city trucks.

Eliana watched, baffled, as he surveyed them then jumped into the back of one. He seemed to find what he was looking for and grabbing two objects, ran back to her. Slightly disturbed that one of the items was a shovel, she backed away, but he walked right past her to the wet patch of dirt and began digging a hole.

"What are you doing?" she asked as it began to sprinkle.

"I'm digging a fucking hole," he grumbled before flinging a scoop of dirt over his shoulder.

"Why?" she asked, and a peal of thunder was heard in the distance.

"Because," he said when the hole was about two and a half feet deep. He tossed the shovel aside and tore open the second item, a long, black plastic bag from which he removed a brown stick that was producing coils of roots. "I'm going to prove to you that just because something old is gone doesn't mean something new, something better isn't coming along." He shoved the plant into the ground and used his hands to pat dirt around the base. "There!" he yelled, brushing his hands off.

"I don't see the point…"

"The point," he said, marching directly up to her and completely invading her space as he stared wide-eyed and sweaty down at her. "That"— he pointed sharply to the plant— "is a fucking apple tree, and in ten years it's going to produce the best fucking apples you've ever tasted, and so help me, Eliana, you're going to be around to eat every single fucking apple it grows!"

Without an ounce of gentleness, he grabbed a handful of her hair and crashed his lips down on hers in a bruising and merciless kiss.

14

They arrived back at the house not a moment too soon as the sky opened up and rain began soaking the ground again. It wasn't the pleasant sort of spring rain that made the air smell fresh and helped to water the budding trees and flowers. It was the sort of rain that raged as though winter was bitter it was being cast aside, so with one spiteful act of revenge, it tore across the earth with her icy shards of water like a final slap in the face.

Eliana shucked her coat and hung it up before kicking her shoes into the corner to dry. She nearly jumped out of her skin when Kye slammed the door behind her. He was in a foul mood. It radiated off him in waves of heat. Without so much as taking off his muddy shoes and cut, he stomped up the stairs and a minute later she heard his bedroom door thump shut as though he'd kicked it.

Sighing herself, she went into the kitchen and started the kettle for a hot cup of tea. The scene in the park had taken them straight through dinner, and her stomach rumbled in hunger. As the water heated, she pulled a few ingredients out of the refrigerator to make chicken and rice. It wasn't gourmet, but it would be warm and filling. The chicken was easy enough as she heated it in the oven with some butter and salt while the rice seeped in the same hot water from the kettle she used to make her tea.

There were no sounds in the house without Kye in the room, and the sounds of the storm grew. Unable to tolerate the silence, she turned on the small kitchen TV to the news. Unsurprisingly, the entire evening segment was focused on the weather and a handsome man in a suit was indicating parts of the coast would be flooding by gesturing to a map that replaced the green screen behind him.

Long after she'd finished her cup of lemon and ginger tea, Eliana still felt chilled. Her clothes weren't wet, but there was a dankness that had sunk into her ever since their argument in the park. She missed her tree. It seemed childish and reminded her of the existential ending of The Giving Tree, but she did.

Her thoughts fell back to what Kye had said, 'It's a

loss, and you cry over losing a friend'. His submission of her attachment to it because of her lack of stability as a child was spot on. Whenever her father had been too drunk to be around or the kids at school had bullied her, she always found her feet trekking back to that tree. She hadn't realized how important it was to her, how many beautiful memories she had of it. Kye was exactly right. She'd lost a friend. She'd lost so many things.

Determined not to feel sorry for herself, Eliana stared into her cup of tea and tried to reassure herself that everything was going to be okay. The tree was an omen that, like it, she would face storms and be torn down. Maybe her life was like that little apple tree Kye had forcefully planted. While she didn't want to be planted there, she was going to make the best of it and, in his words, 'make the best fucking apples anyone had tasted!'

Though the statement was slightly amusing on its own, she couldn't bring herself to smile. It seemed too exhausting to smile at the moment. Not when her heart felt so heavy. Not when images of Kye's fierce expression still plagued her. He'd been livid at her comment about dying and being buried. More than livid, he was positively enraged. It was so unlike him.

While she'd seen glimpses of his temper since their reunion, this was something else entirely. She'd not just pissed him off, she'd offended him. Calm, steady, patient

Kye was angry. Angry at her. Objectively she couldn't blame him. He'd asked her to trust him, she'd declared that she did, then went back on that to sarcastically implicate that not only would he let her die but that he'd be the one to bury her.

Chewing on her bottom lip, she began to feel very sorry for her comments. She'd allowed her melancholy over the loss of her tree to make her reckless with her words, and she'd hurt him. Somehow it did make her feel slightly better knowing that she could affect him, though. It wasn't in her nature to be the emotional one in the room and pitted against Kye's unyielding resolve, she'd often been the tantrum to his temper.

Tucking the leftovers onto a single plate and brewing a second cup of tea, Eliana quietly walked upstairs. The light to Kye's room was on, but when she tried the door, she found it was locked.

"Kye?" she asked, and there was no reply. "Kye?" she called a little louder. Waiting a moment, she still heard no response. "I wanted to say I'm sorry," she said, hoping he wasn't asleep, and her words weren't lost to the oak door. "You were right about what you said. That tree was important to me. I was upset, and I let it get to me. I didn't mean to upset you too." She heard a little shuffling from inside the room, but the door remained closed. "The willow served its purpose," she continued, "when I needed it, it was there. It held me up and sheltered me for a lot of years. I'd like to think the tree died after I left because it knew I didn't need it anymore. I could stand on my own now." She felt a little foolish being so sentimental while staring at a closed door. "Anyway, I made some dinner. It's out here if you want it. I'm going to bed."

Setting the plate and mug down, Eliana padded slowly back to her room. She waited and when she didn't so much as hear his door open, she undressed and went reluctantly to bed with nothing but the memories of his warmth to keep her company.

KYE HAD FINISHED the plate of food and left the dish sitting on the top of the dresser as he jumped into a hot shower. He'd spent the evening brooding in his room, pouring over the plans he'd been working on determined to save Eliana's ungrateful life no matter what. Having sulked for that long, he was cold all the way to his bones and even after eating, he needed to warm up.

Standing under the steaming heat for only a few minutes, he thought he heard something. Turning the water off, he stood silently listening. The storm was raging outside, loud peals of thunder following flashes of lightning, but it was the loud scream that tore him from the shower.

Grabbing his pistol from the end table, he raced down the hallway. A second scream and he kicked Eliana's bedroom door open sure that he was going to find one of Max's goons, if not the man himself, strangling her. Instead, he saw Eliana sitting up in bed, blankets clutched to her chest, and sweat mixing with her tears.

"What? What is it? Did someone hurt you?" he asked, still aiming the gun at anything and everything in the room. Eliana was visibly shaking, and it took a moment for her eyes to focus as she had clearly been abruptly ripped from sleep.

"I was asleep... the thunder it sounded like gunfire, and I thought, in my dream, I was being shot at, and I thought it was... I thought it was real," she choked out. Kye sighed, his adrenaline levels dropping as he lowered his weapon.

"It was only a dream, Eli," he said, rubbing his face. "Just go back to sleep," he tried to encourage from the doorway. When he removed his hand from his eyes, he caught the strange expression on her face that was illuminated by the flash of lightning that momentarily filled the room. Her eyes had been, not on his, but roaming over him in shocked curiosity. Remembering he had been showering, he hadn't so much as wrapped a towel around himself in his haste to get to her.

"Kye..." Her voice was so quiet he could barely hear

it over the rain outside. Another bolt of lightning lit up the room, and this time, her eyes found his. The look wasn't curiosity, and it wasn't shock. It was desire. Raw. Primal. Potent desire. He could taste it in the air.

Placing his gun on the desk, he closed her bedroom door with his foot. The accompanying roll of thunder shook the windows and masked her gasp as he pulled back the covers and climbed into bed next to her. His hair was wet. She felt it brushing against her face when he kissed her. His skin was clammy, but his mouth was hot, and when he leaned over her to press her back into her pillows, she forgot all about her nightmare and lost herself in his touch.

The room was painfully black and had no reprieve save for the sporadic flashes from outside. While this may have been a handicap should they want to see each other, it worked wonders on heightening their other senses. Eliana was keenly aware of the soapy way he smelled, and Kye could taste every delicious inch of her mouth as he devoured it.

They moved without thought, only instinct. Their minds had played this moment thousands of times since they'd first shared this bed ten years ago, so it wasn't any surprise the way Kye slid between her legs so easily. Her thighs gripped his waist salaciously, and his hand dove under the band of her panties to stroke her.

No passing thunderclap covered the sound of the

moan she let out when his finger slid inside her, and Kye felt all traces of cold leave as she poured heat into him from her body. She was groping at him in earnest, begging him with her body to fill her. Kye took hold of her hand that was reaching for his shaft and pinned it above her head.

"Slowly," he whispered into her ear, and she shivered. Her breathing settled, and her bare chest pressed against him as he guided her with gentle rocking motions. Their hips fit together, his erection tucked between her legs, and his mouth moved back to hers. She moaned. Long and slow as his tongue slid in and out of her mouth. His soft lips moved almost lazily against hers.

She had never been kissed like this before. Languid and smoldering, he burned into her as he demonstrated exactly how he was going to take her. To fill her. To claim her. Not soon enough for her liking, but likely in just the right time for her body to be ready, Kye hooked two fingers in her underwear and pulled them off. She lay naked and spread open to him as he gazed down at her. Though neither could see well in the dark, their hands moved with familiarity.

Bowing to her, Kye kissed his way up the inside of her knee to her thigh where he left a trail of small bites that had her toes curling. He paused in his ascent to drag his tongue along her folds, and a cry of pleasure escaped her throat before he was peppering kisses on her stomach then devouring her breasts with more aggression.

"Kye, don't stop this time, please," she pleaded as her shaky hands held onto his shoulders. His mouth left her breast. His face moved up toward hers.

"It's much too late for that," he cooed, and butterflies erupted in her stomach. This was it. No stopping now. He was finally going to…

"Oh God…" she gasped when she felt his tip easing its way inside her. He was moving gradually deeper, and every nerve in her core lit up like a Christmas tree. When he reached her barrier he stopped, unsure. She took the cue and grabbed his ass, bringing him farther into her. The pressure of his cock that deep inside of her made her groan.

"I don't want to hurt you," he said in a strained voice. Her tightness was agony on his throbbing dick that was begging for friction. For movement. For more of her.

"Kye," she said, moving her hands from his backside to his face. Their eyes met. "Hurt me."

As though he'd heard the magical words, he pushed himself entirely into her, and Eliana threw her head back with a loud cry that mixed with the peal of light-ning and thunder that boomed overhead. There was no stopping now as he withdrew halfway and thrust into her a second time. Her legs were clamping down on him almost as if to push him away and simultaneously bring him closer. But he didn't relent. A third and fourth time he pounded into her and by the fifth, she was matching his movements with thrusts of her own.

Certain now that she was alright, Kye pinned her hips to the bed with his and used the spring of the mattress to slam into her. Her breathing was hot against his ear when he buried his face in her neck, and she dug her nails into his back. The pain mixed with the ecstasy of her tight, wet, depth sent him reeling. Knowing he was close to his climax, he angled his hips so his pelvis was pressed directly against her clit. Even between thrusts, he kept constant pressure on her bud.

"Oh my God, I'm going to come," she said frantically. "Kye! Kye!"

"Come on, baby," he said, propping himself up onto his hands. Using the fluid motion of his hips to keep himself inside her, she writhed and curled under him, before her back arched violently, and she bucked her way into an orgasm. "Fuck!" Kye cried when he felt her gushing all over him. The new level of slickness was more than he could stand, and before she'd finished riding the tide of her satisfaction, he was climaxing into his.

The way he filled her sent pulses of pleasure from her stomach to her limbs, and when he finally collapsed onto her, she felt she'd never be able to move again. Her hands began rubbing his back and when he pulled out of her, she shuddered in a mixture of pain, loss, and sensitivity.

"Shh," he whispered against her hair when he tucked her against his side and wrapped an arm around her. "Save your words," he said somehow knowing, even in the dark, she'd opened her mouth to speak. "In a minute, I'm going to do that again. Whatever you want to tell me, wait until after."

Smiling against his side, she began kissing his chest and up to his neck, the heat of her desire no sooner cooling as it began to warm up again.

15

*E*liana felt a warmth on her face before she opened her eyes. Taking a long, slow inhale, she could smell him thick and potent in the air. When her eyes opened, she saw him lying next to her on his back, one arm tucked behind his head, lips parted and breathing short, easy breaths. He looked so peaceful, no lines of worry or age on his face. His hair was unkempt, and his beard was overdue for a trim. He looked perfect.

Lying on her stomach staring at him, she mindlessly chewed on her thumbnail, heat filling her belly when she replayed the night before in her mind. Whatever way she'd imagined being with him, with anyone, he'd surpassed any rich fantasy she'd had. It had felt more natural than she expected. Although she'd felt a little clumsy at first, he'd been steady with his hands and hadn't for a moment let her feel uncertain.

Whether he'd done it intentionally or not, the confidence in the way he'd pushed himself into her, unrelenting, consistent, powerful... he'd instilled that in her with every thrust. Between the darkened room and her heightened desire for him, she'd felt heady and intoxicated, like a kite in a hurricane. He'd been her string. Keeping her grounded and rooted with the sole purpose of letting her fly as high as she needed and bringing her safely back down.

It wasn't hard to maneuver her way between his parted legs and prop herself against his chest. He was starting to wake so she coaxed him the rest of the way out of his slumber with wet kisses on his torso. By the time she reached his neck, his eyes were open, and he was watching her in amusement.

"Good morning," he said in a gravelly voice. She smiled at him before kissing him firmly on the mouth. He tangled a hand in her hair, and she made her intentions known by repeating his act from the night before, rocking her hips against his. His tongue moved into her mouth, and her breathing hitched. He was warm and firm beneath her.

"Mmm," he moaned and inhaled sharply when her hipbone pressed against his forming erection. "Hey now, let a guy brush his teeth first," he teased, and she bit her lip. The way she looked at him with sleepy eyes, he went completely hard. "Come here," he said quietly and took her by the waist, pulling her up until she was straddling him. Her legs were sore and ached when she spread them to fit herself over his lap.

"Kye?" she panted when she felt his dick growing hard and pressing against her core. He kissed her, ridding her of any hesitation. Reaching her hand between them, she guided him toward her entrance and slowly lowered herself. Still swollen from the night before, he filled her painfully at first, every inch of him a mix of sensations. He held her by the hips patiently until she was comfortable, and her body relaxed. At this angle, he was much deeper, his tip directly against her womb that throbbed and pulsated.

"There you go," he murmured against her ear when she began moving up and down. Her body moved without thought. Driven by instinct, it was as though her body knew what she needed even if her mind didn't. Her sounds were more like whimpers, short, high-pitched gasps, and he felt her thighs trembling. Sitting farther up, he wrapped a strong arm around her back, giving her a steady frame to move against.

Eliana braced herself on his broad shoulders, her pace quickening. This new position was exhilarating to her. The feel of him between her legs, the angle of his dick inside her, and the way his pelvis was constantly rubbing her clit every time she moved sent pulses of titillating pleasure through her.

Although everything in him wanted to buck and drive harder into her, he allowed her to set the pace. The freedom she felt taking her pleasure with his body was more erotic than anything he'd experienced before. The way she felt riding him, alternating between rocking back and forth and pounding up and down on him was wild. He made no effort to control her movements, simply content to let her fuck him as her body desired.

It wouldn't take her long to climax, and he knew it. He could tell by how slick she had become, by the way her muscles clenched around his shaft. She was so close he could taste it on her. The moment she lost herself, he cradled her as wave after wave of stimulated nerves wracked her body. She went from completely rigid to limp in his arms and clutching her close, he rolled her over and pressed her firmly into the mattress. Two swift thrusts and he reached his climax. The sweet agony of his orgasm made him feel weak from it.

They lay still for a long moment. His breathing was labored, and he'd collapsed on top of her, face buried in her neck. The full weight of his body on hers was suffocating, and she squirmed. "Kye!" She managed to laugh and pushed his shoulders.

"Sorry," he said, rolling off of her. He lay on his back again, and she draped herself over his chest. Running a hand up and down her back, he kissed the top of her head as she traced small circles on his chest. His skin was smooth, but there was a dusting of dark hair on his chest. A line of it covered his belly button and disappeared beneath the sheets. He caught her wrist when she ran her fingers over it. "Tickles," he muttered with closed eyes.

"So does that," she said, wriggling when his thumb brushed her side. He pressed harder, his hands massaging her now. She made a contented sigh. The warmth of his touch made her instantly relax.

"Eli?" he asked after a drawn-out silence passed between them. She didn't say anything but looked up at him. "Did I hurt you?" His blue eyes were full of concern and to her dismay, a level of guilt.

"Yes," she said, propping her head up on her hand. "I wanted you to," she added before he could respond. He ran a hand over his face, and she grabbed his arm. "Hey, Kye, you did exactly what I wanted you to… and a few things I didn't know I wanted." They both chuckled, and she pressed more firmly against his side. "I enjoyed last night… and this morning."

"For your first time, though…" he started, and she interrupted him with a kiss.

"Despite what you think, not all women want rose petal-covered beds, candlelight, and Marvin Gaye blasting on the stereo." He frowned at her sarcasm. "Kye, do you regret having sex with me?" she asked, holding his chin in her hand and staring into his eyes.

"God, no," he replied quickly. "I just think your first time should have been special."

"Kye, you said it yourself. My first time. You don't get to decide what makes something special to me. I get to decide that. For me," she said, moving a hand to rest on his chest over his heart, "this was very special. I needed it, and I needed it to be with you. Last night was perfect, even if it took ten years to happen. It happened, and I wouldn't change it for anything."

"Are you sure?" He looked so innocent and fragile. If he'd damaged her in any way, he'd never forgive himself. Eliana smiled, feeling almost parental in the way she reassured him with a kiss.

"I'm sure," she said decidedly. "Now, it's time to take a shower then make breakfast." Rising from the bed, she stretched her arms over her head, and Kye lay back enjoying the view of her naked body.

"Are you now?" he asked, grinning from ear to ear. She turned, arms still in the air, eyes playful and mischievous.

"Me?" she asked, looking down at him from the doorway. "I think you mean 'we'," she elaborated. Kye flung the covers aside and caught Eliana before she could leave the room. She shrieked out a laugh as he pulled her over his shoulder and carried her into the bathroom.

* * *

Eliana felt deliciously sore. Every move reminded her of the bliss she'd spent the last several hours experiencing. When she stirred the batter, her abdominal muscles hurt. When she knelt to pull the biscuits out of the oven, her thighs prickled, and when Kye walked behind her toward the stove and paused to kiss the back of her neck, the heat in her region contracted like a cramp.

With the dough in the oven, she wrapped her arms around his waist from behind as he whisked the gravy he was making. He looked over his shoulder at her, and she kissed his cheek.

"That smells good," she said and dipped a serving spoon into the gray liquid before holding it out for her to taste. "Mmm," she said and blew the hot air out of her mouth. "Where did you learn to cook?" she asked and hopped onto the counter next to him. She grimaced for a moment as the strain hurt briefly.

"Picked it up over the years," he said, furrowing his brow when he noticed her discomfort. Turning the heat down on the stove, he crossed to her and placed his hands on her thighs. "Are you sure you…"

"Kye Driscoll"— she wrapped her arms around his neck— "if you keep fussing over me like a broken china doll, I'm going to start to get angry." She pulled him closer, and his hands began massaging her thighs.

"Do you want me to apologize for caring?" he asked as she drew a bare foot up the outside of his leg.

"No," she said, running her hands down his bare chest and tugged at the elastic band of his sweatpants. His hands moved from the silky skin of her legs that were exposed in her jean shorts and to her cheeks where he cradled her face. "Just don't mistake me for fragile."

"You are many things, Eli,"— he kissing her neck— "fragile is not one of them." They held each other for a long moment, his lips moving from one side of her neck to the other. She closed her eyes savoring the feeling.

"Oh shit!" She laughed when the beep from the stove timer interrupted them. Kye stepped back and opened the glass door and removed the cookie sheet. She watched from her perch as he plated two helpings of the biscuits and gravy, setting them on the counter, and she slid onto the barstool next to him.

A comfortable silence passed as they ate and from under the counter, his foot found her leg and began teasingly brushing her soft calf. They'd spent over forty-five minutes in the shower washing each other, learning the other's body, and he'd all too quickly discovered several of her ticklish places that he seized every opportunity to tickle.

They were both startled when the front door opened

and shut. Kye stood and reached for the gun in his jacket pocket, but stopped when he saw Grier rounding the corner. He stopped and stared at Kye who stood shirtless and without socks or shoes before his green eyes moved over to Eliana. She was slightly more modest in jean shorts and a sleeveless shirt.

"What's up?" he asked, feeling as though he'd intruded. Eliana felt on guard, but Kye was perfectly at ease as he sat and continued eating.

"Grab some food," Kye offered and pointed to the two pans on the stovetop. When Grier tossed his cut onto the table next to Kye's, and Eliana noticed the two holstered guns on his hips, she tensed. Kye grabbed her hand under the counter and gave it a squeeze.

"Thanks!" Grier didn't bother grabbing a plate, but instead took a biscuit from the tray, dipped it directly into the saucepan, and shoveled it into his mouth.

"Want some beer to wash that down? I can pour it into a trough for you," Kye asked sarcastically. Grier swallowed the whole mouthful.

"Fuck you, but don't mind if I do," he stated as he opened the fridge and pulled out a bottle.

"Did you drive all the way over here to make a mess and drink my beer?" Kye propped his elbows on the counter. Eliana felt nervous, especially after her last encounter with the man. She knew they were old friends, but Eliana didn't trust anyone from the Demons save for Kye.

"No," Grier said, opening the bottle and taking a swig. When he didn't elaborate, Kye made a sound of annoyance. Grier looked from Kye to Eliana and back. "Haven't been answering your phone," Grier said, "Max is pissed. Wanted to send Dhal and Brutus, but I convinced him I'd get here faster."

"Fuck," Kye said and jumped off the stool. He moved to the table where his phone lay. The charger had come unplugged, and his battery had inadvertently died. He quickly plugged it in and turned it on only to find out he'd missed over a dozen calls. "Battery was dead."

"I figured, but it wasn't like you. Good thing the tracking bracelet was still here; otherwise, Max was apt to think she'd killed you and made a run for it."

"That's bullshit," Eliana interjected. "I've done nothing but cooperate with everything he's wanted. There's no reason for him to suspect I'd do something like that."

"Max suspects everyone of being capable of anything," Grier said in an even tone. "That's why he's in charge."

"What does he want?" Kye asked, flicking through his text messages.

"He wanted an update," Grier said, setting the bottle down. "Now he wants to see you. Just you. She stays here." Eliana looked from Grier to Kye. His jaw had clenched, but he didn't say anything.

"Kye?" she asked when he moved from the table toward the stairs. He gave her the slightest shake of his head when he turned back to look at her. She nodded and turned back to her plate as Kye went upstairs to get dressed. Having lost her appetite, she busied herself by pushing the food from one side of the plate to the other. Grier was staring at her, and she made a point of not looking back at him.

Kye was back in only a few moments, dressed in black pants and a long-sleeved, thermal shirt. He grabbed his cut from the counter and kissed Eliana on the temple. "I'll be back soon," he said with as much confidence as he could. He cast a stern glare at Grier before breezing from the house.

Eliana felt her chest tighten with worry. What was Max's play in all of this? No word for days then, the night they were together, he was suddenly desperate to see Kye? Setting her fork down, she leaned back on the stool.

"What?" she asked Grier who was still staring at her. Folding her arms across her chest, she narrowed her eyes.

"Nothing," he said, taking another swig of beer, "just wondering how long you've been fucking my best friend."

16

"Assuming that's any of your business," Eliana began after gaping at Grier for a long moment, "what makes you think we're 'fucking', as you put it?"

"For one," Grier answered with his arms crossed, "he's wanted to fuck you since you were in high school..."

"That's ancient history."

"Second, the two of you were half-naked when I walked in..."

"We're old friends; it's not weird to be in shorts or pajamas."

"Third, you've got stubble burn and a hickey on your neck."

"I..." Eliana clamped her mouth shut and a hand over her neck where she knew Kye had been paying special attention. Grier, though pleased with himself, maintained a blank expression.

"Exactly," he said, tossing his empty bottle into the sink and retrieving another from the fridge.

"Well, as I said before, it's really not your business," Eliana defended and pushed her plate away, having lost her appetite entirely.

"I just hope it was worth it," Grier said, shutting the refrigerator door harder than necessary.

"I think it was entirely worth it," Eliana said defiantly.

"No surprise you'd think I was talking about you," Grier snapped when he turned to her. Eliana was taken aback. "Despite what you think, princess, your life isn't the only one hanging in the balance. Kye will likely lose everything if Max thinks he's lost his loyalty."

"Kye's a big boy; he makes his own decisions," Eliana argued, feeling the strange need to defend her boyfriend… or lover… or kidnapper, whatever the hell he was to her. "Besides, parting ways with Max is not the worst thing to happen to him."

"Max? Maybe not," Grier agreed verbally, but his tone conveyed he didn't really believe that. "What about the club? Huh? His family?"

"Family?" Eliana asked, patronizingly amused. "A gang of criminals, drug dealers, and traffickers are his family? Good riddance." Eliana jumped when Grier slammed his bottle on the counter. It made a loud clinking sound, and beer foamed out of the open top.

"That just goes to show how ignorant you are," he spat, and Eliana glared. She didn't like being insulted, especially by this thug who had already threatened her. "You march in here on your moral high horse and think you've got everything and everyone figured out, completely inept to what's happening."

"I didn't march in here, I was dragged here," Eliana snapped back, pointing her finger at him. "I don't need to pretend to have the moral superiority to know what your club does. You're the reason there are drugs on the streets, violence, women held in your own compound against their will!"

"You think I don't know that?" Grier asked narrowing his eyes. "There's shit that's been going down long before you came back into the picture. Why do you think Kye is so important? Huh?"

"What are you talking about?" Eliana asked, feeling genuinely confused. Grier sighed, his shoulders slumped, and his temper dissipated as he placed his hands on the counter opposite her. He was quiet for an immeasurable amount of time. His facial expressions conveyed the internal dialogue and debate he was having with himself. Looking up from the counter, his brilliant green eyes bore into her as though he was trying to decide something about her. Eliana raised her eyebrows expectantly.

"Max started dealing in currency other than drugs over a decade ago," Grier said shortly. "That fact didn't sit well with a lot of us."

"People, you mean?" Eliana asked, looking for clarification. "Max started selling people."

"Women mostly, a few kids," Grier answered, and Eliana felt nauseous. "Max had always organized himself well, his closest allies were called the Four Horsemen. He intentionally kept them split. Only two of the men were in on it, Riggs and Shon were the guys leading the traffickers. Shon was killed during the Defector uprising and to our knowledge was never replaced."

"Our?" she asked, looking for clarification. "Who would that be?"

"Those of us who don't believe people are currency," Grier said with a set jaw. "Ironically we have your dad to thank for that."

"What are you talking about?" Eliana asked, entirely perplexed.

"Henry was a transporter. He shuttled around a lot more than car parts and kilos of marijuana," Grier said, looking at her darkly. "Before you wet yourself, Henry didn't know. Transporters weren't allowed to see in the trucks they drove. I don't know what made Henry stop that night, maybe he heard crying or something broke loose, but when he opened the back to check, he found four women chained in the back. He let them go. That's when Hamilton and I caught wind of the secret operations."

"That's why Max had it out for him so bad," Eliana said steadily, though her face had gone brutally pale. "I didn't know, my dad never mentioned anything about that. I guess it explains why he was so determined to keep me away from Kye and the rest of the Demons."

"It took time, but with the distraction of the Defectors, we were able to find the sources and the inner workers. We knew that Max was too big to be taken down from the outside. Cops, FBI, State Patrol would be useless to stop the trafficking without taking down the entire club. We needed someone who could infiltrate the inner circle. Someone who could take down the establishment without causing a civil war or mass arrests of innocent people."

"Kye?" Eliana asked, and Grier nodded. "That's no secret to me. Kye has said multiple times that he was going to change things once Max was out of the picture."

"Well, Kye doesn't know everything," Grier said harshly. "He's too close to it. He's been a pawn just like the rest of them. Do you think Kye knew about the women in that bar? The same women he turned to when he was lonely?"

"Kye would never…"

"Of course he wouldn't!" Grier interrupted. "That's what I'm telling you. Even Max could see that Kye would never agree to that kind of action. That's why Max busied him these last few years running guns to the UK. He even tolerated his little hobby. You."

"Me?"

"Max knew all about his frequent trips to Cambridge to check up on you. You've been Kye's only weakness since he was a prospect. Max wanted that. Fostered that. Let Kye think he was getting away with it because he knew one day he could exploit it if he needed to."

"Is that what Max is doing now?" Even as she asked the question, her hands folded on the counters, she knew the answer. The timing was all too convenient. Max had played things perfectly. This wasn't about Henry dying and passing his debt on to her. This wasn't just about revenge. This was leverage. With Kye due to take over, Max needed to know that even in his death he still had control over the MC. Over Pine Hill. Over Kye. "Fuck," she breathed and covered her face with her hands

"Sucks, doesn't it?" Grier asked as he opened the fridge a third time, pulled out a beer, and set it in front of Eliana.

"Grier," she said, looking up from her hands, "these men I've been finding loopholes for… having released from prison. This isn't just Max's last act of kindness, is it? He's securing business. I've been helping him free kidnappers and rapists."

"Yep," he replied shortly and saluted her with his bottle before taking a swig. "You see, things aren't as black and white as you'd like to think they are. You can look down on us 'criminals, drug dealers' and all-around assholes if you want, but you were caught in the spider's web like the rest of us."

"I'm going to throw up," she declared, hand over her stomach and with no other feasible way to quell her nausea, she downed her beer in one breath. Grier grinned, slightly impressed.

"Kye was poised perfectly to succeed Max. We could have brought all this information to him, and he could have ended it all without any bloodshed."

"Why can't you still do that? Max already told Kye he was going to leave the club to him. Max will be dead soon. Why can't we just wait it out? Just a little longer." Her voice sounded frantic and pleading at this point. Even she could hear the desperation.

"We're long past that," Grier said, placing his hands on the counter again. "Max knows your game, your hold on him. Everything will come to a standstill until Kye proves once and for all his loyalty to the club."

"How does he do that?" Eliana asked, looking up at Grier. The slightly older man leaned his back against the sink and crossed his arms, looking steadily at her. "It's me, isn't it… he has to kill me. That'll be his act of fealty."

"You've been a colossal pain in the ass, but no one can say you're stupid." Eliana felt her hands shaking, and she'd lost feeling in her legs. She desperately wanted to get up, to pace, to make her mind work, but she felt rooted to her seat. Paralyzed was a better word. "Don't worry; he won't do it," Grier interjected, taking her from her thoughts. "As I said, you're his weakness."

"So what happens then? Max orders him to kill me, Kye refuses, and what? He's allowed to just walk away? I doubt that."

"You should," Grier said, as though even the suggestion of it was the stupidest thing he'd ever heard. "If Kye outright refuses, Max will kill him on the spot. He'll hate doing it, but he's not a man who holds on to sentiment. Not this late in the game anyway."

"We can't let that happen!" Eliana had regained her senses and was on her feet. "You-you have to stop Max. We have to kill him!"

"You say that like it's the easiest thing in the world. Just march in his office and put two in his chest. He's got himself holed up in the clubhouse with more security than the president. No, if anyone is going to be killed it needs to be an easier target. Someone… vulnerable."

She froze in place from her pacing when she heard

the clatter on the counter. Turning around, she saw Grier had removed one of his pistols and set it on the counter. She looked from it to his hand to his eyes. "You're here to kill me," she concluded. For some reason, an eerie calm washed over her.

"Those of us who are trying to purify the Demons from soliciting women... they want me to. Kye is our last hope. Without him, Riggs will be named successor, and we're in for another thirty years of hell. Worse, more than likely," Grier explained.

"Kye won't do what you want if you kill me," she said, facing him fully. "When he finds out you shot me, he'll kill you."

"Probably," Grier said, removing his hand from the gun and resting it on his hip. "Then again, I'm not the indispensable one. I've spent years supporting Kye, covering his back, protecting him so that when the time was right he'd be ready to take over and save us from the fate of prospering on slavery. If I die, it's better than things going on as they are. No one life is bigger than this."

"There must be another way," Eliana said in a shaky voice. "You can get me out of town... Kye said he was working on a plan."

"Kye will be at the clubhouse in the next hour. Max is going to give him an ultimatum. If Kye goes in there and is ordered to kill you, we both know how that conversation is going to go. He'll refuse. Max will kill him. Then Dhal, Riggs, or any other member will show up here and kill you anyway. You have to realize, Eliana, you're dead either way." Grier was slow and deliberate in his explanation, and before she knew it, Eliana had hot tears running down her cheeks.

"Why are you telling me all of this? Some sort of mercy killing? Explaining everything so I can live in misery five minutes before I die?" She spat the words with bitterness.

"You deserve to know everything before you make your decision." She was about to ask for clarification, but his answer came before she could ask. He placed his hand on the gun and slid it toward her. Eliana looked at it, now within her reach, and she had to place a hand on the back of the barstool to steady herself.

"You… you wan-want me to kill myself?" she questioned, and her heart slammed inside her chest. Grier looked at her with a mixture of sympathy and consternation. He nodded once. "No. No!" she proclaimed loudly. "I'm not going to kill myself so your little club can survive."

"I'm not asking you to save the club," Grier said over her tirade. "I'm asking you to save Kye. It won't be long until he's in Max's office. He won't walk out of there. We both know that. But if I pick up this phone," he continued to explain as he removed his cell phone, "and

I tell Max that you're dead already. Send him a picture of your lifeless body, then Kye is spared the decision. Kye won't die. You won't be killing yourself— you'll be saving his life."

A short sob burst from Eliana's mouth, and she nearly doubled over the back of the stool. The weight of his words was heavy, and she felt them. She knew Kye would do it. Kye would let Max kill him before he'd let anything happen to her. He'd promised as much a hundred times. She wanted to protect him too. Was this how to do it? Wasn't there another way? She ran a hand over her face. Even if there had been another plan, they were out of time.

Grier, at this moment, was checking his watch. How long had it been since Kye left? Was he already in the office? At this very moment, Kye could be on his knees with a gun to his head, being forced to agree to murder her or die. She sobbed again when she thought of it and knew Kye would die. Without knowing it, he'd walked out the door, and she'd never see him again. Their first night together would be their last.

"You love him," Grier said, coming around to her side of the counter and hesitantly placing a hand on her shoulder. "If you love him, you have to do this. You have to do it now. Before Kye gets to the compound."

Her hand was shaking as she reached for the gun. Grier stepped aside and let her take it. It was heavier than she imagined. She'd never fired a gun before; the metal was cold. The fleeting thought of turning the gun on Grier and killing him instead crossed her mind, but what would that solve? She'd be free, but Kye would be dead.

"Tell him…" she choked out as she looked at Grier. "T-tell him… tell him I love him," she pleaded, and Grier nodded. He took another step back. Placing the barrel end against her temple she took a steadying breath and gave Grier one last look before squeezing her eyes shut…

…and pulled the trigger.

Bang.

It was difficult to drive his bike with all the knots in his stomach. Kye was mentally kicking himself for allowing his cell phone battery to die. He'd been so engrossed with Eliana and their steamy night that he had completely lost himself and forgotten about the delicate situation they were in. Both he and Eliana were under the proverbial microscope, and his lapse in judgment would cost them. Assuming he could talk his way out of it, at the very least Max would bolster security at the house. There was no way around that.

The roads were still rain-soaked from the onslaught of rain they'd had these last several days, and the black clouds on the horizon foreshadowed another stormy night. The unpaved road that led to the clubhouse was all mud puddles and loose gravel to the point Kye considered walking. He braved it, however, and by the time he pulled into the courtyard and to the parking lot, his pants were soaked from the knee down and the visor of his helmet was caked.

The impending storm was nothing compared to the rumbling of onlookers. Something was going down. Kye could taste it in the air, and all eyes were on him as he crossed the yard toward the main building. He'd listened to the increasingly irate voicemails that had been left on his phone from the night before, seen the text messages. Max was in a mood, and when that happened, everyone was on edge.

Although he knew he should hurry, Kye couldn't escape the dread that overwhelmed him, and he trekked slowly through the wreck room, past the gym equipment, the TV screens and into the back hallway. His boots left muddy footprints behind him, and the rubber squeaked on the tile floors.

When he reached the lobby waiting room that led to Max's office, he was morose, if not surprised, to see the increase in security. In addition to Dhal's four-man team, there were two others placed at the door and another near the entrance to Max's office. Dhal greeted him with a snarl.

"Picked a fine time to disappear," the gruff man said, both hands resting on the pistols on his hips.

"I didn't disappear; I was working. Not that my business has fuck-all to do with you," Kye said confidently.

"You think you're any better than the rest of the lot out there?" Dhal asked, stepping into Kye's face. "Think Max won't personally order your balls in a jar to decorate his office if you piss him off? You're nothing."

"You need to spend less time thinking about my balls and more time shining your shoes," Kye said darkly. "First thing I do when I'm in charge is kick your useless ass to the curb."

"We'll see about that," Dhal challenged and snapped his fingers to the guard at the door. "Let him in."

The man at the door to Max's office wordlessly turned the knob and swung the door in. Kye entered, fully aware that Dhal was at his back, and he heard the door shut behind him. Max was seated in his armchair and an enforcer stood at his back brandishing an automatic rifle. From the look of Max, he didn't need to question the reason for all the attention.

"Nice of you to grace us with your presence," Max croaked. His voice was only slightly smoother than the sound of breaking glass, and he had to hold a handkerchief to his mouth. The man must have suffered a minor stroke. While the right side of his face still held the strength to glare, the left side was partially paralyzed.

"Max," Kye said, rushing forward. He must have

moved too quickly because the man behind the chair flinched. "God, I had no idea…"

"Save your pity," Max said holding a hand up. "Never thought I'd live to feel so fucking decrepit," he grumbled as he stood. On top of the slacking face, he now brandished a limp. "You wanna tell me where the fuck you've been? I swear to God, if you tell me you spent the last twelve hours in pussy town, Yaakov is going to put a bullet in your head." Kye glanced at the tall man behind the desk.

"It was a stupid mistake," Kye said, looking back at Max. "I didn't go dark on purpose; cell phone went to shit on me that's all."

"Mmhmm," Max said, unconvinced.

"Check the tower records if you need, Max. I was in the same location. It's just that my battery died."

"You think I give two fucks about your cell phone?" Max asked, and Kye had to admit, in his haste he should have thought of a better excuse. "We're on the final stretch of a legacy, the end of the Max Strong dynasty, and where is my right hand? My protégé? Balls deep in his high school sweetheart!"

"That's not exactly…"

"Don't lie to me, boy," Max said sternly, and Kye clamped his mouth shut. Looking minutes from death and the man still intimidated him. "I want to know where we stand. Tell me once and for all where your loyalties lie."

"They're with you, Max. With the Demons. Always has been, always will be."

"Prove it."

"Prove it?" Kye asked, feeling his ire rise. "You're fucking kidding me, right?" Max, for the briefest moment, had a look of surprise. "I've done everything you ever asked me to do, and I've made you a rich man doing it. You wanna know the truth? Yeah, I fucked her. God, I bent her over the counter and fucked her until she couldn't walk." Yaakov chuckled. "I fucked her because you told me to. I fucked her, got it out of my system, and that's the end of it. You're pissed because I went dark for less than a day. You've been dead ass silent for almost a week. The fuck did you want me to do?"

"Watch your tone with me, boy," Max said, pointing a threatening finger at him. "I don't owe you an explanation."

"Actually, you do," Kye replied. "You name me second, yet you're keeping things from me. Shit, Max, you look like you've had a stroke, and I seem to be the last person to know. You want me to carry on your legacy, keep the club going strong? You've got me undermined before I ever take authority. Like it or not, Max, once you're dead, this club isn't going to hang on to your every word anymore. You want to present a strong, united front. This is the fucking wrong way to do it."

"Hmm," Max said with a contemplative growl. He tapped a finger to his temple. "You think I don't know that?" Max asked, and his head jerked in a slight spasm. "Since we're telling the truth here, I've been reconsidering my decision."

"Why?"

"The girl."

"If you were so worried about her, you never should have brought her back into the picture," Kye argued.

"She had her hold on you, boy. Here or there doesn't matter. You've always been divided. Torn. A man at war with himself. It's about as productive as you taking a piss in the wind."

"Whether you name me successor or not, I'm a Demon through and through," Kye said firmly. Max, with his lopsided face, grinned and clapped Kye on the shoulder.

"You've made friends in the club, son. The Demons like you. Look up to you. Hell, a lot of them fear you. But you're crazy if you think after me there's a future for you here. Say I name Riggs King, what's the first thing you think he'll do?"

"Fuck his way through Jez's?"

"Don't get smart with me," Max said, but he chuckled. "If not Riggs, what about Dhal. What do you think he'll do first?"

"You'd really name Dhal?"

"I'd name anyone I thought wasn't going to fuck things up," Max barked, and for the first time, Kye could hear the desperation in his voice. Kye gripped Max by his good shoulder and stared the man in the eyes.

"Max," he said, stepping closer and resting his forehead against the older man's. "You're scared. You don't show it, but I know you are. It's a fucking waste the way things are ending for you. I've let you down. I've worried you. I am still the man you raised. I am still the leader you made me into. You have to trust me. Trust me now, to honor you. To represent you. To keep your legacy safe. I am your man."

"I know, son," Max said, gripping Kye's arm. A tear leaked from Max's left eye, and he sniffled before pulling away. "But I need to know. Once and for all. You choose me, you choose this club over everything." Before Kye could ask how, Max was crossing back to his desk. "Kill her."

"Kill… Eliana?"

"Do you know another 'her' I could be referring to?" Max asked sarcastically. "She's a threat. I've seen her casework. She's good, and she knows too much. Plus, she's pissed. We let her go, she'll make it her life work to take us down."

"So… we don't let her go," Kye said, turning to face him. "We keep her. Believe me, the condition I left her in, she's a submissive, purring kitten." Yaakov chuckled again, and Max glared at him. "She already quit her job, left the law firm. She's got other priorities now."

"She's a woman. She might be sucking your dick today, but that bitch has teeth, and she'll use them. I've decided. As my final order, I want her dead. I want you to kill her. If you don't do it, I've got a list of men who will. Your buddy, Grier? He's at the top of that list." Kye felt his hands ball into fists. "Didn't realize he was on my payroll, did you? Had him keeping his eye on you all these years, making sure my grooming was working."

"Grier has always had his own priorities, I never claimed to have his loyalty above his allegiance to you."

"No, no you didn't," Max agreed, sitting back in his chair. "What's your answer, son?" Max asked, getting back to the point.

"I can use her."

"That's not good enough," Max said, and using his good hand, gestured to Dhal. Kye felt a hand on his shoulder from behind, and his knees were kicked out from underneath him as he was forced to the ground. The cocking of a pistol sent shivers up his spine. "I want her dead. I want you to kill her."

"Max, don't do this," Kye pleaded, and Dhal pressed a

hard boot to his back, pinning him to the ground. Kye was unable to move let alone reach his gun.

"You have one more chance," Max said slowly, and Dhal grabbed Kye's ponytail, yanking his head back and drawing him to his knees. Standing from his seat once again, Max walked over to the kneeling Kye and took the gun Dhal extended to him. The moment the barrel of it was aimed directly at him, images of Eliana flashed across his mind.

Had he known their first time together would be their last, he wouldn't have bothered with breakfast. He'd have laid in that bed with her until they'd burned the house down with them inside. Refusing to close his eyes, he set his jaw and prepared to meet his maker.

Then a phone rang.

Max, still holding the gun aimed at Kye, looked behind him at Dhal. "Sorry, pres, its Grier," Dhal said. He heard the phone beep. "What?" Dhal snapped. "Fuck... pres, you'd better hear this."

"What is it?" Max asked as though he wasn't about to murder Kye. Dhal had to hold the phone up to Max's ear as his left hand was so contorted it would never be able to grip it. "Make it fast," Max said into the phone. The muffled sounds of Grier talking on the other end reached Kye, but he dare not move a muscle. "She what? How the fuck did that happen?" Max snapped. Kye felt panic creep over him. Max looked from Dhal back to

Kye. "Did you do this?" he asked, and Kye remained silent. "I want proof," Max said into the phone. A moment later it chimed, and Dhal pressed a button that lit up the screen. "Well, I'll be damned… when you said you left her in a state, I didn't think you'd go this far."

"Nicely done," Dhal goaded and held the phone so Kye could see the picture. Everything in him stopped functioning when he saw the picture of Eliana. "I didn't think you had it in you."

"I don't like being fucked with," Max said and gestured for Kye to stand. "You tell me you want to keep her alive, then I see this? I guess I should be proud. You're testing me the way I tested you." Kye stood, but he didn't remember even thinking to do it. He was numb. "Grier said he found her like that. Sure as hell isn't his handiwork."

"No…" Kye said and found his throat had gone dry. His brain was operating on pure instinct now. Go with the story. Keep it simple until he had more answers. He hadn't left Eliana like that. Not laying there on the kitchen floor… "I did what you asked, Max," Kye said, fighting back tears.

"I need more proof than a picture, son," Max said, and Kye nodded ever so slightly.

"I'll take her to the reservoir," he suggested. "Put her in one of the levees…"

"Good, do it," Max said shortly. "Then I want you

back here. And, Kye," he said when the dark-haired man had reached the door, "don't forget to charge your phone."

Kye had to force himself to walk slowly. Each step was deliberate. Timed. Careful. He knew he was still being watched, but everything in him wanted to tear through that place and get back to her. He'd seen the picture. Eliana laying on the kitchen floor covered in blood. His throat was constricting to the point he couldn't breathe.

The moment he reached his bike, he didn't bother with his helmet. The mud would obscure his vision anyway. Kicking the bike to life, it roared down the soaked backstreet away from the clubhouse. When he finally pulled back onto the open road, he was off like a rocket.

The only thing he could think was that Grier had killed her. Had it been one of Max's men, Kye wouldn't have walked out of the office alive. How could he do that? How could he betray him after all they'd been through? Kye's furious grip on the handlebars tightened, and tears mixed with the rain that was starting to shower.

He'd find out what happened to Eliana, and whoever was responsible would pay. With their life.

DARK DESIRES
~ A billionaire dark romance series ~
Dark Desire
Dark Rules
Dark Secret
Dark Time
Dark Truth

BARRE TO BAR
~ A billionaire second chance series ~
Dancing With Lies
Dancing With Temptation
Dancing With Doubt
Dancing With Guilt
Dancing With Redemption

TWISTED INTENTION
~ A billionaire revenge romance series ~
Twisted Beauty
Twisted Love
Twisted Fate

Mafia's Obsession
~ A hot mafia romance series ~
Mafia's Dirty Secret
Mafia's Fake Bride
Mafia's Final Play

Screaming Demons
~ An MC romance series full of suspense ~
Rough Start
Rough Ride
Rough Choice
Rough Patch
Rough Return
Rough Road
Rough Trip
Rough Night
Rough Love

Standalone Contemporary Romance
Billionaire in Vegas
Billionaire Hunt

Billionaire's Game
Billionaire Retreat
Billionaire On Air
A Chance To Love
Somebody To Love
Not Mine To Love

Check out Summer's entire collection at
www.summercooper.com/books

ABOUT SUMMER COOPER

Thank you so much for reading. Without you, it wouldn't be possible for me to be a full-time author. I hope you enjoy reading my books as much as I do writing them.

Besides (obviously!) reading and writing, I also love cuddling my dogs, shouting at Alexa, being upside down (aka Yoga) and driving my family cray-cray!

Get in touch at
hello@summercooper.com
www.summercooper.com

facebook.com/summercooperauthor
instagram.com/summercooperauthor
goodreads.com/summercooper
bookbub.com/profile/summer-cooper

www.ingramcontent.com/pod-product-compliance
Lightning Source LLC
Chambersburg PA
CBHW031238210726
48287CB00003B/812